PUFFIN BOOKS

Editor: Kaye Webb

THE PUFFIN BOOK OF SALT-SEA VERSE

Now Fiddler's Green is a place I've heard tell
Where fishermen go if they don't go to hell
Where the weather is fair and the dolphins do play
And the cold coast of Greenland is far far away.

CHORUS
Dress me up in me oil-skin and jumper,
– No more on the docks I'll be seen,
Just tell me old ship-mates I'm takin' a trip, mates,
And I'll see you some day in Fiddler's Green.

JOHN CONOLLY

Charles Causley, who compiled for us *The Puffin Book of Magic Verse*, has spent almost all his life near, or on, the sea, and has now collected together a truly magnificent and far-ranging anthology of poems, reflecting that 'many-faced, many-voiced ̶ ̶ ̶ ̶ ̶ ̶ ̶ ̶ ured element'. His choice includes themes as di ̶ ̶ ̶ ̶ ̶ ̶ ̶ ̶ ̶ ̶ ̶ ̶ ̶ rs, naval engagements, shipwrecked mar ̶ ̶ ̶ ̶ ̶ ̶ ̶ ̶ ̶ ̶ ̶ ̶ ̶ ̶ ls, and the poets he introduces ̶ ̶ ̶ ̶ ̶ ̶ ̶ ̶ ̶ ̶ ̶ ̶ ̶ ̶ ̶ e Ancient Greeks to the ̶ ̶ ̶ ̶ ̶ ̶ ̶ ̶ ̶ ̶ ̶ ̶ ̶ ̶ ̶ Patten and William Pes ̶ ̶ ̶ ̶ ̶ ̶ ̶ ̶ ̶ ̶ ̶ ̶ ̶ ̶ ̶ sea, or hates it, will find ̶ ̶ ̶ ̶ ̶ ̶ ̶ ̶ ̶ ̶ ̶ ̶ ̶ to begin at the beginning. T ̶ ̶ ̶ ̶ ̶ ̶ ̶ ̶ ̶ ̶ ̶ ck, Storm and Disaster', or 'I Do Like ̶ ̶ ̶ ̶ ̶ ̶ ̶ ̶ de', or 'Findings and Keepings', and start the ̶ ̶ ̶ ̶ ̶ ̶ ̶ ̶

Charles Causley, himself ̶ ̶ ̶ ̶ ̶ ̶ ̶ ̶ nguished poet, has included only three of his own poems here, but if you want to know more of his work, his books of verse include *Figgie Hobbin* (shortly to be published in Puffin), *Figure of 8* and *The Tail of the Trinosaur*.

The Puffin Book of Salt-Sea Verse

Compiled and Introduced
by
Charles Causley

Illustrated by
Antony Maitland

PUFFIN BOOKS

Puffin Books, Penguin Books Ltd, Harmondsworth, Middlesex, England
Penguin Books, 625 Madison Avenue, New York, New York 10022, U.S.A.
Penguin Books Australia Ltd, Ringwood, Victoria, Australia
Penguin Books Canada Ltd, 2801 John Street, Markham, Ontario, Canada L3R 1B4
Penguin Books (N.Z.) Ltd, 182–190 Wairau Road, Auckland 10, New Zealand

—

First published 1978
Published simultaneously in hardback by Kestrel Books

—

This collection copyright © Charles Causley, 1978
Illustrations copyright © Antony Maitland, 1978
All rights reserved

—

Made and printed in Great Britain
by Richard Clay (The Chaucer Press) Ltd,
Bungay, Suffolk
Set in Monotype Ehrhardt

*Acknowledgements are included in the Acknowledgements
section, which is on pages 269–72. The Acknowledgements section is an
extension of the copyright page.*

CONTENTS

5

CONTENTS

ON THE BEACH

FINDINGS AND KEEPINGS

CONTENTS

I DO LIKE TO BE BESIDE THE SEASIDE

HARBOUR AND ISLAND, CAPE AND CLIFF

FISHING AND FISHERFOLK

CONTENTS

CONTENTS

IN DEEP

SEA-CHANGES

CONTENTS

LOVERS FALSE AND LOVERS TRUE

DREAMERS, SOLITARIES AND SURVIVORS

SHIPWRECK, STORM AND DISASTER

CONTENTS

WRECKERS, INVADERS, PIRATES AND PRISONERS

BATTLES AND ENGAGEMENTS

CONTENTS

TO KAYE WEBB

INTRODUCTION

ALL the poems in this selection of 'salt' verse have something
to do with what Shakespeare, in *Henry V*, calls 'the wild and
wasteful ocean'. It seems to me a happy accident that salt is
also the ancient symbol of purity, vigour, wit, strong love, and –
perhaps most important of all – incorruptibility and eternal
life: all qualities associated with the best of poetry, and of every
kind of art.

The core of the anthology, and the subject of its opening
section, is the sea itself: the many-faced, many-voiced, many-
natured element that R. S. Thomas, a poet of our own day,
sees in a few short lines as successively a child's plaything, a
whip, a fighter, one who scrubs and scours, a rock-grinding
monster, a passionate lover, but also

> ... Mostly
> It is a stomach, where bones,
> Wrecks, continents are digested.   (*page* 23)

An American poet of the last century, Emily Dickinson,
walking early on the beach with her dog, communicates – gently
but powerfully – that growing sense of unease most of us feel
when confronted by the ocean's beauty and casual strength, its
awful indifference to our insignificant selves. She returns home

with a slightly quicker step, one feels, than that with which she set out:

> And he, he followed close behind;
> I felt his silver heel
> Upon my ankle, then my shoes
> Would overflow with pearl,
>
> Until we met the solid town.
> No one he seemed to know
> And bowing with a mighty look
> At me, the sea withdrew.   (*page* 25)

Apart from the years of the Second World War (which I spent as a lower-decker in the Royal Navy) I have lived almost the whole of my life in Cornwall. Here, it is impossible to be more than a score of miles from the sea; and – for my part, certainly – one is hardly ever unaware of its almost all-encroaching presence. As a child, the first seas I saw were those that exploded on the sawing rocks and perpendicular cliffs of North Cornwall: the wrecking coast of the Victorian parson-poet Robert Stephen Hawker (pp. 222 and 231); and the first chillingly realistic comment on the sea I came across in print was in a school edition of Charles Dickens's *David Copperfield*. It is a passage I have carried in my memory ever since. Young David and Little Em'ly are picking up stones on the beach at Yarmouth:

'You're quite a sailor, I suppose?' I said to Em'ly. I don't know that I supposed anything of the kind, but I felt it an act of gallantry to say something; and a shining sail close to us made such a pretty little image of itself, at the moment, in her bright eye, that it came into my head to say this.

'No,' replied Em'ly, shaking her head, 'I'm afraid of the sea.'

'Afraid!' I said, with a becoming air of boldness, and looking very big at the mighty ocean. '*I* an't!'

'Ah! but it's cruel,' said Em'ly. 'I have seen it very cruel to some of our men. I have seen it tear a boat as big as our house all to pieces.'

Since childhood, then, my view of the sea has been respectful, but – of course – by no means an entirely sober and serious one. For several years before and during the First World War, my mother lived in the red-cliffed little seaside resort of Teignmouth in South Devon (where, incidentally, the poet John Keats nursed his sick younger brother Tom in 1818). Here, in her day, nothing delighted my mother more than to watch the pierrots in the concert-party. From them, she learned the popular songs of the time, and often sang them to me as an alternative to 'Twinkle, twinkle, little star' and 'Baa, baa, black sheep'. So, very early on, I found myself familiar not only with the immortal 'I do like to be beside the seaside' (p. 73), but also with Fred Earle's song about seaweed – the poor man's barometer and magic charm:

> It tells you if it's going to rain, or if it's going to snow.
> And with it anyone can tell just what he wants to know. (*page* 75)

Although, terrifyingly, a beach could easily become Kevin Crossley-Holland's 'stadium of roaring stones' (p. 49), it was also the damp stage for the performances of the sand artist with his masterpieces made of materials as short-lived as spun sugar or ice-cream. His apparent unconcern that his creations – mermaids, crocodiles, sea-beasts, in coloured sand and bright pebbles – might well be swallowed by the advancing tide at first amazed but later comforted me. Evidently, I thought at the end, he was supremely confident that his powers of creativity would be with him still the next day: a powerful example, this, for all creators.

On a much more northerly beach than mine, and with a man of slightly different methods, James Kirkup sees the sand artist, very properly, as a god and as a poet in his own right:

> From the sea's edge he draws his pail
> of bitter brine, and bears it carefully
> towards the place of first creation. (*page* 77)

The sea, of course, inspired the poet and singer long before Odysseus (or Ulysses) and Noah were sailors, and Peter was a fisherman. Almost all of us have strong feelings of love or fear or hatred for the ocean: and sometimes a strange mixture of all three. Not surprisingly, then, many good poems have arisen out of these strong feelings: for art cannot take root in attitudes of indifference or apathy.

Perhaps a major source of the fascination that the sea exerts on us is that which sets the Greek sea-god Poseidon apart from most of his fellows. In a brilliant study called *The Sea in English Literature*,* published over half a century ago, the Cornish writer Anne Treneer points out that many have been forced to conclude that 'to Poseidon . . . belongs that most ungodlike of attributes – he is shifty, . . . the sea is ungenerous, not to be trusted for a moment, without character or will of its own, reflecting the sky, following the moon, and driven by the wind.'

This always remembered, few are able to resist, all the same, its myriad beauties, its extraordinary qualities of perpetual change and self re-creation, its unsleeping and even unwinking power. The pathos, the very human story, contained in the lines of the Greek poet Isidorus speak to us as clearly across two thousand years as on the day the poem was written:

> Eteocles was I, whom hope of gain
> In ocean trade lured from a farmer's home;
> I crossed the ridges of the Tyrrhene main
>   And, ship and all, plunged headlong to my doom,
> Crushed by a sudden squall; for different gales
> Blow on the threshing-floor, and on the sails.   (*page* 227)

Its sentiment is true of all times and places, ancient or modern. The wry words of Isidorus are almost interchangeable with those of John Pudney, a poet of our own time, who – like his Greek predecessor – captures precisely the quiet, authentic, slightly self-deprecating voice of man, the eternal seafarer:

*University Press of Liverpool/Hodder & Stoughton, 1926.

Some say it isn't deep
But it's deep enough for me.
Don't write no address on my grave
But the Mediterranean Sea . . .

Ships you never heard of,
Fleets that went down in thunder:
And them old shipmates from all the wars
Sharing the Mediterranean plunder.   (*page* 159)

A share of plunder that, in a very real sense, will never be lost to us as long as tales are told, poems read, songs sung, will be found, I hope, in the pages that follow. The secret dream of every poet is to write a line that lasts for ever, and the voice of Rafael Alberti (p. 149) is a subtle and prudent reminder of this ever-present hope:

If my voice should die on land,
take it to sea-level
and leave it on the shore.

Launceston, Cornwall   CHARLES CAUSLEY

THE SEA ITSELF

WORD

The word bites like a fish.
Shall I throw it back free
Arrowing to that sea
Where thoughts lash tail and fin?
Or shall I pull it in
To rhyme upon a dish?

STEPHEN SPENDER

THE SEA

They wash their hands in it.
The salt turns to soap
In their hands. Wearing it
At their wrists, they make bracelets
Of it; it runs in beads
On their jackets. A child's
Plaything? It has hard whips
That it cracks, and knuckles
To pummel you. It scrubs
And scours; it chews rocks
To sand; its embraces
Leave you without breath. Mostly
It is a stomach, where bones,
Wrecks, continents are digested.

R. S. THOMAS

TELL ME, TELL ME, SARAH JANE

Tell me, tell me, Sarah Jane,
    Tell me, dearest daughter,
Why are you holding in your hand
    A thimbleful of water?
Why do you hold it to your eye
    And gaze both late and soon
From early morning light until
    The rising of the moon?

Mother, I hear the mermaids cry,
    I hear the mermen sing,
And I can see the sailing-ships
    All made of sticks and string.
And I can see the jumping fish,
    The whales that fall and rise
And swim about the waterspout
    That swarms up to the skies.

Tell me, tell me, Sarah Jane,
    Tell your darling mother,
Why do you walk beside the tide
    As though you loved none other?
Why do you listen to a shell
    And watch the billows curl,
And throw away your diamond ring
    And wear instead the pearl?

Mother I hear the water
    Beneath the headland pinned,
And I can see the sea-gull
    Sliding down the wind.

I taste the salt upon my tongue
As sweet as sweet can be.

Tell me, my dear, whose voice you hear?

It is the sea, the sea.

CHARLES CAUSLEY

I STARTED EARLY, TOOK MY DOG

I started early, took my dog,
And visited the sea.
The mermaids in the basement
Came out to look at me

And frigates in the upper floor
Extended hempen hands,
Presuming me to be a mouse
Aground upon the sands,

But no man moved me till the tide
Went past my simple shoe
And past my apron and my belt
And past my bodice too,

And made as he would eat me up
As wholly as a dew
Upon a dandelion's sleeve;
And then I started too

And he, he followed close behind;
I felt his silver heel
Upon my ankle, then my shoes
Would overflow with pearl,

Until we met the solid town.
No one he seemed to know
And bowing with a mighty look
At me, the sea withdrew.

EMILY DICKINSON

A SEA DIRGE

There are certain things – as, a spider, a ghost,
    The income-tax, gout, an umbrella for three –
That I hate, but the thing that I hate the most
    Is a thing they call the Sea.

Pour some salt water over the floor –
    Ugly I'm sure you'll allow it to be:
Suppose it extended a mile or more,
    That's very like the Sea.

Beat a dog till it howls outright –
    Cruel, but all very well for a spree:
Suppose that he did so day and night,
    That would be like the Sea.

I had a vision of nursery-maids;
    Tens of thousands passed by me –
All leading children with wooden spades,
    And this was by the Sea.

Who invented those spades of wood?
  Who was it cut them out of the tree?
None, I think, but an idiot could –
  Or one that loved the Sea.

It is pleasant and dreamy, no doubt, to float
  With 'thoughts as boundless, and souls as free':
But, suppose you are very unwell in the boat,
  How do you like the Sea?

'But it makes the intellect clear and keen' –
  Prove it! Prove it! How can that be?
'Why, what does "B sharp" (in music) mean,
  If not "the natural C"?'

What! Keen? With such questions as 'When's high
    tide?'
  'Is shelling shrimps an improvement to tea?'
'Were donkeys intended for man to ride?'
  Such are our thoughts by the Sea.

There is an insect that people avoid
  (Whence is derived the verb 'to flee').
Where have you been by it most annoyed?
  In lodgings by the Sea.

If you like your coffee with sand for dregs,
  A decided hint of salt in your tea,
And a fish taste in the very eggs –
  By all means choose the Sea.

And if, with these dainties to drink and eat,
  You prefer not a vestige of grass or tree,
And a chronic state of wet in your feet,
  Then – I recommend the Sea.

For *I* have friends who dwell by the coast –
  Pleasant friends they are to me!
It is when I am with them I wonder most
  That anyone likes the Sea.

They take me a walk: though tired and stiff,
  To climb the heights I madly agree;
And, after a tumble or so from the cliff,
  They kindly suggest the Sea.

I try the rocks, and I think it cool
  That they laugh with such an excess of glee,
As I heavily slip into every pool
  That skirts the cold cold Sea.

Once I met a friend in the street,
  With wife, and nurse, and children three:
Never again such a sight may I meet
  As that party from the Sea.

Their cheeks were hollow, their steps were slow,
  Convicted felons they seemed to be:
'Are you going to prison, dear friend?' 'Oh, no!
  We're returning from the Sea!'

                                    LEWIS CARROLL

NORTH SEA OFF CARNOUSTIE

You know it by the northern look of the shore,
by the salt-worried faces,
by an absence of trees, an abundance of lighthouses.
It's a serious ocean.

Along marram-scarred, sandbitten margins
wired roofs straggle out to where
a cold little holiday fair
has floated in and pitched itself
safely near the prairie of the golf course.
Coloured lights are sunk deep into the solid wind,
but all they've caught is a pair of lovers
and three silly boys.
Everyone else has a dog.
Or a room to get to.

The smells are of fish and of sewage and cut grass.
Oystercatchers, doubtful of habitation,
clamour 'weep, weep, weep' as they fuss over
scummy black rocks the tide leaves for them.

The sea is as near as we come to another world.

But there in your stony and windswept garden
a blackbird is confirming the grip of the land.
'You, you,' he murmurs, dark purple in his voice.

And now in far quarters of the horizon
lighthouses are awake, sending messages –
invitations to the landlocked,
warnings to the experienced,
but to anyone returning from the planet ocean,
candles in the windows of a safe earth.

ANNE STEVENSON

THE SEA

A SONG

The sea is jewelled luxury
to him who, on his holiday,
lies on sand beneath the sun
and plays among the waves for fun.

Chorus And thoughts I hardly understand
disturb me as, upon the land,
I hear the waves rush down the strand.

To him who, when the dance is over,
walks with arms about his lover,
sea and stars together press
to illustrate their happiness.

But I have heard a woman shout
and rockets call the lifeboat out,
when sea with neither fuss nor noise
stifled the breath of careless boys.

It has no cruelty nor sense
of humour nor indifference.
Before men came it washed this shore,
it will when men come here no more.

JAMES SIMMONS

THE LAST CHANTEY

'And there was no more sea'

Thus said the Lord in the Vault above the Cherubim,
  Calling to the Angels and the Souls in their degree:
    'Lo! Earth has passed away
    On the smoke of Judgment Day.
  That Our word may be established shall We gather
      up the sea?'

Loud sang the souls of the jolly, jolly mariners:
  'Plague upon the hurricane that made us furl and flee!
    But the war is done between us,
    In the deep the Lord hath seen us –
  Our bones we'll leave the barracout', and God may
      sink the sea!'

Then said the soul of Judas that betrayèd Him:
  'Lord, hast Thou forgotten Thy covenant with me?
    How once a year I go
    To cool me on the floe?
  And Ye take my day of mercy if Ye take away the sea.'

Then said the soul of the Angel of the Off-shore Wind:
  (He that bits the thunder when the bull-mouthed
      breakers flee):
    'I have watch and ward to keep
    O'er Thy wonders on the deep,
  And Ye take mine honour from me if Ye take away the
      sea!'

Loud sang the souls of the jolly, jolly mariners:
  'Nay, but we were angry, and a hasty folk are we!
    If we worked the ship together
    Till she foundered in foul weather,
  Are we babes that we should clamour for a vengeance
    on the sea?'

Then said the souls of the slaves that men threw over-
    board:
  'Kennelled in the picaroon a weary band were we;
    But Thy arm was strong to save,
    And it touched us on the wave,
  And we drowsed the long tides idle till Thy Trumpets
    tore the sea.'

Then cried the soul of the stout Apostle Paul to God:
  'Once we frapped a ship, and she laboured woundily.
    There were fourteen score of these,
    And they blessed Thee on their knees,
  When they learned Thy Grace and Glory under Malta
    by the sea!'

Loud sang the souls of the jolly, jolly mariners,
  Plucking at their harps, and they plucked unhandily:
    'Our thumbs are rough and tarred,
    And the tune is something hard –
  May we lift a Deepsea Chantey such as seamen use at
    sea?'

Then said the souls of the gentlemen-adventurers –
  Fettered wrist to bar all for red iniquity:
    'Ho, we revel in our chains
    O'er the sorrow that was Spain's;
  Heave or sink it, leave or drink it, we were masters of
    the sea!'

Up spake the soul of a gray Gothavn 'speckshioner –
  (He that led the flenching in the fleets of fair Dundee):
    'Oh, the ice-blink white and near,
    And the bowhead breaching clear!
  Will Ye whelm them all for wantonness that wallow
    in the sea?'

Loud sang the souls of the jolly, jolly mariners,
  Crying: 'Under Heaven, here is neither lead nor lee!
    Must we sing for evermore
    On the windless, glassy floor?
  Take back your golden fiddles and we'll beat to open
    sea!'

Then stooped the Lord, and He called the good sea up
    to Him,
  And 'stablishèd his borders unto all eternity,
    That such as have no pleasure
    For to praise the Lord by measure,
  They may enter into galleons and serve Him on the
    sea.

Sun, Wind, and Cloud shall fail not from the face of it,
  Stinging, ringing spindrift, nor the fulmar flying free;
    And the ships shall go abroad
    To the Glory of the Lord
  Who heard the silly sailor-folk and gave them back
    their sea!

RUDYARD KIPLING

barracout': barracuda: a large, greedy fish
picaroon: pirate ship
frapped: bound up tightly with rope
Gothavn 'speckshioner: an official from Gothavn in North Greenland who
  inspected whalers
flenching: cutting up and slicing (as with the blubber of a whale)

EVENING ON CALAIS BEACH

It is a beauteous evening, calm and free,
  The holy time is quiet as a Nun
  Breathless with adoration; the broad sun
Is sinking down in its tranquillity;
The gentleness of heaven broods o'er the Sea:
  Listen! the mighty Being is awake,
  And doth with his eternal motion make
A sound like thunder – everlastingly.
Dear Child! dear Girl! that walkest with me here,
  If thou appear untouch'd by solemn thought,
  Thy nature is not therefore less divine:
Thou liest in Abraham's bosom all the year;
  And worshipp'st at the Temple's inner shrine,
  God being with thee when we know it not.

WILLIAM WORDSWORTH

liest in Abraham's bosom: to rest peacefully in death

CREATURES
OF SEA,
LAND AND
SKY

LITTLE FISH

The tiny fish enjoy themselves
in the sea.
Quick little splinters of life,
their little lives are fun to them
in the sea.

D. H. LAWRENCE

RIDDLE

Mermaids' tears, crusted with time,
Wept long ago, now gather them early,
Trailing beards and trailing slime,
Little morsels, salt and pearly.

JOHN FULLER

Answer: oysters

CRAYFISH FACTS 1–4

i can't help but admire the crayfish
with its hide like crackling.

its antennae are red like scalded
cocktail grasses.

you couldnt pierce the crayfish
with a bowie spike.

it lives in a beautiful fluid garden.
its eyes are very small.

WILLIAM PESKETT

37

LOBSTERS IN THE WINDOW

First, you think they are dead.
Then you are almost sure
One is beginning to stir.
Out of the crushed ice, slow
As the hands of a schoolroom clock,
He lifts his one great claw
And holds it over his head;
Now, he is trying to walk.

But like a run-down toy;
Like the backward crabs we boys
Splashed after in the creek,
Trapped in jars or a net,
And then took home to keep.
Overgrown, retarded, weak,
He is fumbling yet
From the deep chill of his sleep

As if, in a glacial thaw,
Some ancient thing might wake
Sore and cold and stiff
Struggling to raise one claw
Like a defiant fist;
Yet wavering, as if
Starting to swell and ache
With that thick peg in the wrist.

I should wave back, I guess
But still in his permanent clench
He's fallen back with the mass
Heaped in their common trench

Who stir, but do not look out
Through the rainstreaming glass,
Hear what the newsboys shout,
Or see the raincoats pass.

W. D. SNODGRASS

THE LEMMINGS

Once in a hundred years the Lemmings come
Westward, in search of food, over the snow;
Westward until the salt sea drowns them dumb;
Westward, till all are drowned, those Lemmings go.

Once, it is thought, there was a westward land
(Now drowned) where there was food for those starved
  things,
And memory of the place has burnt its brand
In the little brains of all the Lemming kings.

Perhaps, long since, there was a land beyond
Westward from death, some city, some calm place
Where one could taste God's quiet and be fond
With the little beauty of a human face;

But now the land is drowned. Yet still we press
Westward, in search, to death, to nothingness.

JOHN MASEFIELD

THE WHALE

His Nature

The whale's a fish: of all that be,
He's the hugest in the sea.
You could well observe his size
If you saw him with your eyes
Afloat. Indeed, you'd think you saw
An island based on the sea-floor.
This mighty monster of the sea,
When hungry, gapes enormously,
And from his throat his breath is hurled,
The sweetest smell in all the world.
So other fishes towards him go,
Whose scent and taste delight him so,
He savours them in joy awhile:
They have no notion of his guile.
And then the whale shuts his jaw
And sucks those fishes to his maw.
Thus he deceives the fishes small:
The big he cannot hold at all.
The whale lives on the ocean bed
In health and safety, free from dread,
Till summer and winter furiously
Conflicting, storm and stir the sea.
The monster cannot dwell therein
When that season's gales begin,
So turbid is the ocean-floor,
Nor can he bear it any more.
The water thrashes ceaselessly
While that storm is on the sea.

The ships tossed on this tempest high
(Which long to live and hate to die)
Look about them, see the whale,
And thereupon an island hail.
They look on it with great delight,
And pull to it with all their might.
At once they go about to moor,
And everyone proceeds ashore.
They kindle then with steel and stone
A blaze upon this marvellous one:
They warm themselves, and eat and drink:
He feels the fire and makes them sink.
He dives at once to the ocean bed,
And, though unwounded, they are dead.

Explication

Mighty the Devil in strength and in will,
Like witches in witchcraft, doing ill.
With hunger and thirst he makes men a-fire
And burn with many a sinful desire.
His breathing allures, and men come to his face:
Whatever men follow him end in disgrace.
The small fish are those whose faith is unsure.
The big can resist the strength of his lure.
The big, I assert, are those steady and whole,
Whose true faith is perfect in body and soul.

Who listens to the Devil's lore
At last shall find it grieves him sore:
Who hopes by it to prosper well
Shall follow him to darkest hell.

ANONYMOUS
Translated from the Middle English by Brian Stone

THE SHARK

A treacherous monster is the Shark
He never makes the least remark.

And when he sees you on the sand,
He doesn't seem to want to land.

He watches you take off your clothes,
And not the least excitement shows.

His eyes do not grow bright or roll,
He has astounding self-control.

He waits till you are quite undrest,
And seems to take no interest.

And when towards the sea you leap,
He looks as if he were asleep.

But when you once get in his range,
His whole demeanour seems to change.

He throws his body right about,
And his true character comes out.

It's no use crying or appealing,
He seems to lose all decent feeling.

After this warning you will wish
To keep clear of this treacherous fish.

His back is black, his stomach white,
He has a very dangerous bite.

LORD ALFRED DOUGLAS

THE MALDIVE SHARK

About the Shark, phlegmatical one,
Pale sot of the Maldive sea,
The sleek little pilot-fish, azure and slim,
How alert in attendance be.
From his saw-pit of mouth, from his charnel of maw
They have nothing of harm to dread
But liquidly glide on his ghastly flank
Or before his Gorgonian head;
Or lurk in the port of serrated teeth
In white triple tiers of glittering gates,
And there find a haven when peril's abroad,
An asylum in jaws of the Fates!
They are friends; and friendly they guide him to prey,
Yet never partake of the treat –
Eyes and brains to the dotard lethargic and dull,
Pale ravener of horrible meat.

HERMAN MELVILLE

phlegmatical: sluggish; not easily excited
Maldive: the coral Maldive Islands in the Indian Ocean
Gorgonian: hideous; in Greek mythology, the Gorgons were three sisters
  with snakes for hair, hands of brass, teeth like the tusks of the wild boar,
  their bodies covered with impenetrable scales, and with the power of
  turning all on whom they gazed to stone

THE SEA BIRD

Walking along beside the beach
where the Mediterranean turns in sleep
under the cliff's demiarch

through a curtain of thought I see
a dead bird and a live bird
the dead eyeless, but with a bright eye

the live bird discovered me
and stepped from a black rock into the air –
I turn from the dead bird to watch him fly,

electric, brilliant blue,
beneath he is orange, like flame,
colours I can't believe are so,

as legendary flowers bloom
incendiary in tint, so swift he
searches about the sky for room,

towering like the cliffs of this coast
with his stiletto wing
and orange on his breast:

he has consumed and drained
the colours of the sea
and the yellow of this tidal ground

till he escapes the eye, or is a ghost
and in a moment has come down
crept into the dead bird, ceased to exist.

KEITH DOUGLAS

Written at Nathanya, Palestine (now Israel) in 1942; Douglas was killed
fighting in Normandy in 1944, three days after the beginning of the
Second Front. He was 24.

THE HERON

The cloud-backed heron will not move:
He stares into the stream.
He stands unfaltering while the gulls
And oyster-catchers scream.
He does not hear, he cannot see
The great white horses of the sea,
But fixes eyes on stillness
Below their flying team.

How long will he remain, how long
Have the grey woods been green?
The sky and the reflected sky,
Their glass he has not seen,
But silent as a speck of sand
Interpreting the sea and land,
His fall pulls down the fabric
Of all that windy scene.

Sailing with clouds and woods behind,
Pausing in leisured flight,
He stepped, alighting on a stone,
Dropped from the stars of night.
He stood there unconcerned with day,
Deaf to the tumult of the bay,
Watching a stone in water,
A fish's hidden light.

Sharp rocks drive back the breaking waves,
Confusing sea with air.
Bundles of spray blown mountain-high
Have left the shingle bare.
A shipwrecked anchor wedged by rocks,

Loosed by the thundering equinox,
Divides the herded waters,
The stallion and his mare.

Yet no distraction breaks the watch
Of that time-killing bird.
He stands unmoving on the stone;
Since dawn he has not stirred.
Calamity about him cries,
But he has fixed his golden eyes
On water's crooked tablet,
On light's reflected word.

VERNON WATKINS

THE CORMORANT

A lone black crag stands offshore,
Lashed by the flying spray. Gorged from his fishing-
    foray
With long hooked beak and greenish glistering eye,
A cormorant, like a heraldic bird,
Spreads out dark wings, two tattered flags, to dry.

JOHN HEATH-STUBBS

ON THE BEACH

STONES BY THE SEA

Smooth and flat, grey, brown and white,
Winter and summer, noon and night,
Tumbling together for a thousand ages,
We ought to be wiser than Eastern sages.
But no doubt we stones are foolish as most,
So we don't say much on our stretch of coast.
Quiet and peaceful we mainly sit,
And when storms come up we grumble a bit.

JAMES REEVES

The term 'Eastern sages' usually refers to the Wise Men who brought gifts to the Infant Jesus. The Wise Men of Greece (*c.* 600 B.C.–500 B.C.) were also known as the Seven Sages, and to each was attributed some such maxim or motto as 'Know thyself', 'Consider the end', etc.

A BEACH OF STONES

That stadium of roaring stones,
The suffering. O they are not dumb things,
Though bleached and worn, when water
Strikes at them. Stones will be the last ones;
They are earth's bones, no easy prey
For breakers. And they are not broken
But diminish only, under the pestle,
Under protest. They shift through centuries,
Grinding their way towards silence.

KEVIN CROSSLEY-HOLLAND

STONE SPEECH

Crowding this beach
are milkstones, white
teardrops; flints
edged out of flinthood
into smoothness chafe
against grainy ovals,
pitted pieces, nosestones,
stoppers and saddles;
veins of orange
inlay black beads:
chalk-swaddled babyshapes,
tiny fists, facestones
and facestone's brother
skullstone, roundheads
pierced by a single eye,
purple finds, all
rubbing shoulders:
a mob of grindings,
groundlings, scatterings
from a million necklaces
mined under sea-hills, the pebbles
are as various as the people.

CHARLES TOMLINSON

BY THE SEA

Why does the sea moan evermore?
  Shut out from heaven it makes its moan,
It frets against the boundary shore:
All earth's full rivers cannot fill
The sea, that drinking thirsteth still.

Sheer miracles of loveliness
   Lie hid in its unlooked-on bed:
Anemones, salt, passionless,
Blow flower-like – just enough alive
To blow and multiply and thrive.

Shells quaint with curve or spot or spike,
   Encrusted live things argus-eyed,
All fair alike yet all unlike,
Are born without a pang, and die
Without a pang, and so pass by.

CHRISTINA ROSSETTI

argus-eyed: watchful; sharp-sighted

In Greek legend, Argus, a monster with a hundred eyes, was set by the
jealous Hera to watch her rival Io. But Argus was charmed into sleep by
the music of Hermes, and killed by him. Hera then transferred the eyes
to the tail of the peacock.

THE SHORE

If it were not for the weak
rose of white white foam
which it remotely invents,
who would tell me
that it moved its chest while
breathing, that it's
alive with an impulse inside,
that it craves the entire earth
and the blue quiet July sea?

PEDRO SALINAS
Translated from the Spanish by Willis Barnstone

ONCE BY THE PACIFIC

The shattered water made a misty din.
Great waves looked over others coming in,
And thought of doing something to the shore
That water never did to land before.
The clouds were low and hairy in the skies,
Like locks blown forward in the gleam of eyes.
You could not tell, and yet it looked as if
The shore was lucky in being backed by cliff,
The cliff in being backed by continent;
It looked as if a night of dark intent
Was coming, and not only a night, an age.
Someone had better be prepared for rage.
There would be more than ocean-water broken
Before God's last *Put out the Light* was spoken.

ROBERT FROST

LITTORAL

The skyline smoke, bulwarks of sand:
His tunic creased from side to side
The blue god creeps upon the land
Relentlessly with every tide.

Inscrutably, with every tide
The blue god meets prosaic land,
His ruffled tunic drifting wide,
His torn lace tossed upon the sand.

CHRIS WALLACE-CRABBE

The blue god: the Roman Neptune or the Greek Poseidon, god of the sea

SONG ON CAESARIA BEACH

'Come again next summer,'
Or words like that
Hold my life
Take away my days
Like a line of soldiers
Passing over a bridge
Marked for exploding.
'Come again next summer,'

Who hasn't heard these words?

But who comes again?

YEHUDA AMICHAI
Translated from the Hebrew by Assia Gutmann

SONG AT THE TURNING OF THE TIDE

O do not let the levelling sea,
the rub and scrub of the wave,
scour me out or cover me
with sand in a shallow grave.

But let my image, like a rock
contemptuous of the tide's attack,
shift no inch at the green shock
and glisten when the wave springs back.

JON STALLWORTHY

THE TIDE RISES, THE TIDE FALLS

The tide rises, the tide falls,
The twilight darkens, the curlew calls;
Along the sea-sands damp and brown
The traveller hastens toward the town;
    And the tide rises, the tide falls.

Darkness settles on roofs and walls,
But the sea in the darkness calls and calls;
The little waves, with their soft white hands,
Efface the footprints in the sands,
    And the tide rises, the tide falls.

The morning breaks; the steeds in their stalls
Stamp and neigh, as the hostler calls;
The day returns; but nevermore
Returns the traveller to the shore,
    And the tide rises, the tide falls.

HENRY WADSWORTH LONGFELLOW

THE DROWNED SPANIEL

The day-long bluster of the storm was o'er:
The sands were bright; the winds had fallen asleep:
And, from the far horizon, o'er the deep
The sunset swam unshadow'd to the shore.
High up the rainbow had not pass'd away,
When roving o'er the shingly beach I found
A little waif, a spaniel newly drown'd;
The shining water kiss'd him as he lay.
In some kind heart thy gentle memory dwells,
I said, and, though thy latest aspect tells

Of drowning pains and mortal agony,
Thy master's self might weep and smile to see
His little dog stretch'd on these rosy shells,
Betwixt the rainbow and the golden sea.

CHARLES TENNYSON TURNER

THE BANISHED DUKE OF GRANTHAM

Three youths went a-fishing
    Down by yon seaside,
And they saw a dead body
    Cast up by the tide.

This youth said to that youth,
    These words I heard him say:
' 'Tis the banished Duke of Grantham,
    And the tide's on its way!'

They took him up to Portsmouth,
    To the place where he was known,
And from thence up to London,
    The place where he came from.

They drew out his bowels,
    They stretchèd out his feet,
And they balmèd his body
    With spices fresh and sweet.

They set him in his coffin,
    They raised him from the ground,
Nine lords followed after,
    While the trumpets did sound.

O, black was their mourning,
And white were their wands,
And yellow were the flamboys
That they held in their hands.

He lies betwixt two towers,
He lies in cold clay,
And the Royal Queen of England
Goes weeping away.

ANONYMOUS

flamboys: flambeaus or flambeaux; torches, each made of several thick
wicks dipped in beeswax

There are many versions of this ballad, the original central character of
which is perhaps William De La Pole (1396–1450), Duke of Suffolk. On
his way to a five-year banishment to France, his ship was intercepted and
he was beheaded. His body was washed ashore near Dover. The incident
of Queen Margaret's tears is also mentioned in Shakespeare's play *Henry
VI, Part 2*, at the beginning of Act IV, Scene 4.

WHAT COUNTRY, FRIENDS, IS THIS?

(SCENE: THE SEA-COAST)
Enter Viola, Captain, and Sailors

VIOLA   What country, friends, is this?
CAPTAIN   This is Illyria, lady.
VIOLA   And what should I do in Illyria?
         My brother he is in Elysium.
         Perchance he is not drown'd: what think
              you, sailors?
CAPTAIN It is perchance that you yourself were sav'd.
VIOLA   O my poor brother! and so perchance may
              he be.

CAPTAIN   True, madam: and, to comfort you with
                     chance,
                  Assure yourself, after our ship did split,
                  When you and those poor number sav'd
                     with you
                  Hung on our driving boat, I saw your
                     brother,
                  Most provident in peril, bind himself, –
                  Courage and hope both teaching him the
                     practice, –
                  To a strong mast that liv'd upon the sea;
                  Where, like Arion on the dolphin's back,
                  I saw him hold acquaintance with the waves
                  So long as I could see.

WILLIAM SHAKESPEARE
From *Twelfth Night*

Arion: Greek poet and musician of the seventh century B.C.; legend says
that sailors, planning to murder him for his treasure, allowed him first
to sing; that he then sprang (or was thrown) overboard, and that a dol-
phin, attracted by the music, carried him on its back safely to shore

JUST THEN ANOTHER EVENT

Just then another event, the most alarming yet,
Befell us wretches, muddling still further our hooded
   minds.
Laocoon, whom we'd elected by lot as Neptune's priest,
Was sacrificing a great bull at the official altar,
When over the tranquil deep, from Tenedos, we saw –
Telling it makes me shudder – twin snakes with
   immense coils
Thrusting the sea and together streaking towards the
   shore:

Rampant they were among the waves, their blood-red crests
Reared up over the water; the rest of them slithered along
The surface, coil after coil sinuously trailing behind them.
We heard a hiss of salt spray. Next, they were on dry land,
In the same field – a glare and blaze of bloodshot eyes,
Tongues flickering like flame from their mouths, and the mouths hissing.
Our blood drained away at the sight; we broke and ran. The serpents
Went straight for Laocoon. First, each snake knotted itself
Round the body of one of Laocoon's small sons, hugging him tight
In its coils, and cropped the piteous flesh with its fangs. Next thing,
They fastened upon Laocoon, as he hurried, weapon in hand,
To help the boys, and lashed him up in their giant whorls.
With a double grip round his waist and his neck, the scaly creatures
Embrace him, their heads and throats powerfully poised above him.
All the while his hands are struggling to break their knots,
His priestly headband is spattered with blood and pitchy venom;

All the while, his appalling cries go up to heaven –
A bellowing, such as you hear when a wounded bull
  escapes from
The altar, after it's shrugged off an ill-aimed blow at
  its neck.
But now the twin monsters are gliding away and
  escaping towards
The shrine of relentless Minerva, high up on our
  citadel,
Disappearing behind the round of the goddess' shield,
  at her feet there.
Then, my god! a strange panic crept into our people's
  fluttering
Hearts: they argued Laocoon had got what he deserved
For the crime, the sacrilege of throwing his spear at the
  wooden
Horse and so profaning its holiness with the stroke.

VIRGIL
From *The Aeneid*, Book II
Translated from the Latin by C. Day Lewis

Laocoon: a Trojan priest of Apollo; while sacrificing to Poseidon he and
  his two sons were squeezed to death by great serpents
The Aeneid: an epic Latin poem in 12 books telling of the legendary
  adventures of the Trojan hero Aeneas after the fall of Troy

DISCOVERY

There was an Indian, who had known no change,
   Who strayed content along a sunlit beach
Gathering shells. He heard a sudden strange
   Commingled noise; looked up; and gasped for speech.
For in the bay, where nothing was before,
   Moved on the sea, by magic, huge canoes,
With bellying cloths on poles, and not one oar,
   And fluttering coloured signs and clambering crews.

And he, in fear, this naked man alone,
   His fallen hands forgetting all their shells,
His lips gone pale, knelt low behind a stone,
   And stared, and saw, and did not understand,
Columbus's doom-burdened caravels
   Slant to the shore, and all their seamen land.

SIR JOHN SQUIRE

Columbus in the *Santa Maria*, accompanied by the little caravels *Pinta* and *Niña*, the whole party numbering about 120 men, arrived in the Bahamas from Spain in 1492.

FINDINGS AND KEEPINGS

BEACHCOMBER

Monday I found a boot –
Rust and salt leather.
I gave it back to the sea, to dance in.

Tuesday a spar of timber worth thirty bob.
Next winter
It will be a chair, a coffin, a bed.

Wednesday a half can of Swedish spirits.
I tilted my head.
The shore was cold with mermaids and angels.

Thursday I got nothing, seaweed,
A whale bone,
Wet feet and a loud cough.

Friday I held a seaman's skull,
Sand spilling from it
The way time is told on kirkyard stones.

Saturday a barrel of sodden oranges.
A Spanish ship
Was wrecked last month at The Kame.

Sunday, for fear of the elders,
I sit on my bum.
What's heaven? A sea chest with a thousand gold coins.

GEORGE MACKAY BROWN

elders: in certain Protestant churches, those who help the minister manage
church affairs

George Mackay Brown was born in the Orkney Islands.

THE BLACK PEBBLE

There went three children down to the shore,
    Down to the shore and back;
There was skipping Susan and bright-eyed Sam
    And little scowling Jack.

Susan found a white cockle-shell,
    The prettiest ever seen,
And Sam picked up a piece of glass
    Rounded and smooth and green.

But Jack found only a plain black pebble
    That lay by the rolling sea,
And that was all that ever he found;
    So back they went all three.

The cockle-shell they put on the table,
    The green glass on the shelf,
But the little black pebble that Jack had found,
    He kept it for himself.

                                        JAMES REEVES

SHELL TO GENTLEMAN

It's very difficult for two shells to speak
Freely together. Each listens to its own sea call.
It remains for the pearl-diver or the peddler of the
    antique
To say with firmness: 'Same sea, after all.'

                                        T. CARMI
                Translated from the Hebrew by Dom Moraes

THE SHELL

And then I pressed the shell
Close to my ear,
And listened well.

And straightway, like a bell,
Came low and clear
The slow, sad, murmur of far distant seas

Whipped by an icy breeze
Upon a shore
Wind-swept and desolate.

It was a sunless strand that never bore
The footprint of a man,
Nor felt the weight

Since time began
Of any human quality or stir,
Save what the dreary winds and wave incur.

And in the hush of waters was the sound
Of pebbles, rolling round;
For ever rolling, with a hollow sound:

And bubbling sea-weeds, as the waters go,
Swish to and fro
Their long cold tentacles of slimy grey:

There was no day;
Nor ever came a night
Setting the stars alight

To wonder at the moon:
Was twilight only, and the frightened croon,
Smitten to whimpers, of the dreary wind

And waves that journeyed blind. . .
And then I loosed my ear – Oh, it was sweet
To hear a cart go jolting down the street.

JAMES STEPHENS

SO; LIFT THERE

Enter two Servants, with a chest

FIRST SERVANT So; lift there.
CERIMON   What is that?
FIRST SERVANT   Sir, even now
  Did the sea toss upon our shore this chest:
  'Tis of some wrack.
CERIMON   Set it down: let's look
     upon't.
SECOND GENTLEMAN 'Tis like a coffin, sir.
CERIMON   Whate'er it be,
  'Tis wondrous heavy. Wrench it open straight;
  If the sea's stomach be o'ercharg'd with gold,
  'Tis a good constraint of fortune it belches upon us.
SECOND GENTLEMAN 'Tis so, my lord.
CERIMON How close 'tis caulk'd and bitumed!
  Did the sea cast it up?
FIRST SERVANT I never saw so huge a billow, sir,
  As toss'd it upon shore.

CERIMON Come, wrench it open.
Soft! it smells most sweetly in my sense.
SECOND GENTLEMAN A delicate odour.
CERIMON As ever hit my nostril. So, up with it.
O you most potent gods! what's here? a corse!
FIRST GENTLEMAN Most strange!
CERIMON Shrouded in cloth of state: balm'd and
entreasur'd
With full bags of spices! A passport too!
Apollo, perfect me i' the characters! *Reads from a
scroll*
'Here I give to understand
If e'er this coffin drive a-land,
I, King Pericles, have lost
This queen worth all our mundane cost.
Who finds her, give her burying;
She was the daughter of a king:
Besides this treasure for a fee,
The gods requite his charity!'

WILLIAM SHAKESPEARE
From *Pericles, Prince of Tyre*

ARCHAIC APOLLO

Dredged in a net the slender god
Lies on deck and dries in the sun,
His head set proudly on his neck
Like a runner's whose race is won.

On his breast the Aegean lay
While the whole of history was made;
That long caress could not warm the flesh
Nor the antique smile abrade.

He is as he was, inert, alert,
The one hand open, the other lightly shut,
His nostrils clean as holes in a flute,
The nipples and navel delicately cut.

The formal eyes are calm and sly,
Of knowledge and joy a perfect token –
The world being caught in the net of the sky
No hush can drown a word once spoken.

WILLIAM PLOMER

abrade: wear away

A HERMIT'S DREAM

I think it was I who found this thing –
stone-white among shell and shingle,
small as a thimble. If I picked it up,
I would have turned it in my palm, discovering
the holes that dripped cold water.
I would have held a tiny skull.

Like a bird's egg, oval,
thin as egg-shell, how the sea
which is not delicate had left it whole
perplexes me – it may not have come far
but it is clean as though it came from history,
and fine, as if an oriental craftsman

shaped it from white jade
and gave it to the sea.
It lets through light and has two sharp
parabolas of teeth – a carnivore's.
The jaw still works. There is
no trace of flesh, the eyes

were rainbows briefly, then spilled.
Empty, dry, and unlike conches, soundless,
it has no rightful place, no other bones.
It is like a hermit's dream
of being clean at last,
his body shared out to the elements,

become a vessel for some tide to fill.
I am no hermit and I do not dream,
but cupping it face-down in my palm
I think with my warmth
it could hatch out
a creature I would recognize, with wings,

a thing the sea and I would satisfy.
Turning it face upward I can choose
between a relic and a piece of time.
I watch a bone. I watch ancestors in its face.

MICHAEL SCHMIDT

parabola: a section of a cone

RIDDLE

Woman on a wheel,
Ship on the sea,
Eddystone Lighthouse,
What can it be?

ANONYMOUS

Answer: An old-fashioned penny

THE TIDES TO ME, THE TIDES
TO ME

The tides to me, the tides to me
  come dancing up the sand:
when the waves break I lean to take
  each one by the hand.

The tides from me, the tides from me
  roll backward down the shore.
I do not mind, for I shall find
  a thousand and one more.

GEORGE BARKER

I DO LIKE TO BE BESIDE
THE SEASIDE

Everyone delights to spend their summer's holiday
Down beside the side of the silvery sea.
I'm no exception to the rule, in fact, if I'd my way
I'd reside by the side of the silvery sea.
But when you're just the common or garden Smith or
  Jones or Brown
At bus'ness up in town
You've got to settle down
You save up all the money you can till summer comes
  around,
Then away you go
To a spot you know, where the cockle shells are found.

  Chorus
Oh! I do like to be beside the seaside
I do like to be beside the sea
I do like to stroll upon the Prom, Prom, Prom,

73

Where the brass bands play
Tiddely om pom pom!
So just let me be beside the seaside
I'll be beside myself with glee
And there's lots of girls beside,
I should like to be beside,
Beside the seaside!
Beside the sea!

Timothy went to Blackpool for the day last Easter-tide
To see what he could see by the side of the sea.
Soon as he reach'd the station there, the first thing he
  espied
Was the Wine Lodge door, stood open invitingly.
To quench his thirst, he toddled inside, and called out
  for a 'wine',
Which grew to eight or nine
Till his nose began to shine.
Said he 'What people see in the sea I'm sure I fail to see!'
So he caught the train
Back home again,
Then to his wife said he!

  Chorus

Oh! I do like to be beside the seaside *etc.*

William Sykes the burglar, he'd been out to work one
  night
Filled his bag with jewels, cash and plate.
Constable Brown felt quite surprised when William
  hove in sight.
Said he 'The hours you're keeping are far too late'
So he grabbed him by the collar and lodged him safe
  and sound in jail.

Next morning looking pale
Bill told a tearful tale.
The judge said, 'For a couple of months I'm sending
   you away!'
Said Bill, 'How kind! Well! if you don't mind
Where I spend my holiday,'

  Chorus

Oh! I do like to be beside the seaside *etc.*

JOHN A. GLOVER-KIND

John A. Glover-Kind also wrote the music for these verses. In his book on music-hall songs of 1840–1920, *Sweet Saturday Night* (1967), Colin Mac-Innes tells us that when the comedian Mark Sheridan sang it, he 'wore his uniform of stove-pipe hat, frock coat, motoring gloves, grotesquely bell-bottomed trousers, and battered brolly which he thumped on the stage to reinforce his delivery'.

SEAWEED

Last summer time I went away to Dover by the sea.
And thought I'd like to bring a bunch of seaweed home
   with me.
It tells you if it's going to rain, or if it's going to snow.
And with it anyone can tell just what he wants to know.

With my seaweed in my hand I got into the train;
All the pubs were closed when I got out again.
I couldn't get a drink – with thirst I thought I'd die,
And as soon as I touched my seaweed I knew it was
   going to be dry.

FRED EARLE

This music-hall song was also composed and originally sung by Fred Earle.

75

NEWSFLASH

In a dawn raid
early this morning
Gendarmes arrested
a family of four
found bathing
on a secluded beach
outside Swansea.

Later in the day
tracker dogs
led German police officers
to the scene of a picnic
near Brighton.
Salmonpaste sandwiches
and a thermos of tea
were discovered.
The picnickers however
escaped.

ROGER MCGOUGH

ON THE LIDO

On her still lake the city sits
While bark and boat beside her flits,
Nor hears, her soft siesta taking,
The Adriatic billows breaking.

ARTHUR HUGH CLOUGH
From *At Venice*

THE SAND ARTIST

On the damp seashore
above dark rainbows of shells, seaweed, seacoal,
the sandman wanders, seeking for a pitch.

Ebb tide is his time. The sands are lonely,
but a few lost families
camp for the day on its Easter emptiness.

He seeks the firm dark sand of the retreating waves.
– With their sandwiches and flasks of tea, they
lay their towels on the dry slopes of dunes.

From the sea's edge he draws his pail
of bitter brine, and bears it carefully
towards the place of first creation.

There he begins his labours. Silent,
not looking up at passing shadows
of curious children, he moulds his dreams.

Not simple sandcastles, melting as they dry,
but galleons, anchors, dolphins, cornucopias of fish,
mermaids, Neptunes, dragons of the deep.

With a piece of stick, a playing card
and the blunt fingers of a working man
the artist resurrects existence from the sea.

And as the returning tide takes back its gifts,
he waits in silence by his pitman's cap
for pennies from the sky.

JAMES KIRKUP

77

THE LUGUBRIOUS,
SALUBRIOUS SEASIDE

The dogs' tails tick like metronomes,
Their barks encore the sticks you throw,
The sallow clouds yawn overhead,
The sagging deck-chairs yawn below.
I wish I had my marble clock
To race those minatory tails,
Or the fire-buckets at the Bank
To shame those proud enamelled pails,
Those wooden spades that dig the mind,
Unearthing memories of spades
When we were the protagonists
Flaunting down juvenile parades.
I hide my face in magazines
While children patronise the grave
Of mariners, while bathing girls
Deign to illuminate the wave.
That never-satisfied old maid, the sea,
Rehangs her white lace curtains ceaselessly.

LOUIS MACNEICE

minatory: threatening; menacing

I WOKE THIS MORNING TO A
SOLITARY TERN

I woke this morning to a solitary tern
Carried my shoes down the stairs
Not to wake the children
Dressed, and went out.

78

The sky was light blue, the cottages white.
I counted the church clock strike six.
The steady surf, and several gulls.

On the beach the tide was out
And a young girl was writing in the sand
With one foot, in careful letters, Tom.
Then she walked bare-footed, like the girls from
The West of Ireland. The Back Road was empty.
The roofs with dew. Everything else was still.

Along the front the breeze was cold
And in the cheap shop's window I saw myself
The centre of a large green ball:
A little silly, with the harbour curving
Behind me until it vanished
Into a green glass sea and a green glass sky.

Then the sun came out.
And I saw the policeman who passed me, stop.
And at the bus-stop, a driver.
And going up the hill an old man with a cane
Turned and stared at the sea and the sky.

We stood there – from the different levels
Of this terraced town – and in our silence
Paid the necessary acknowledgement.

NORMAN LEVINE

'The Back Road' is in St Ives, Cornwall.

DELECTABLE DUCHY

Where yonder villa hogs the sea
Was open cliff to you and me.
The many-coloured cara's fill
The salty marsh to Shilla Mill.
And, foreground to the hanging wood,
Are toilets where the cattle stood.
The mint and meadowsweet would scent
The brambly lane by which we went;
Now, as we near the ocean roar,
A smell of deep-fry haunts the shore.
In pools beyond the reach of tides
The Senior Service carton glides,
And on the sand the surf-line lisps
With wrappings of potato crisps.
The breakers bring with merry noise
Tribute of broken plastic toys
And lichened spears of blackthorn glitter
With harvest of the August litter.
Here in the late October light
See Cornwall, a pathetic sight,
Raddled and put upon and tired
And looking somewhat over-hired,
Remembering in the autumn air
The years when she was young and fair –
Those golden and unpeopled bays,
The shadowy cliffs and sheep-worn ways,
The white unpopulated surf,
The thyme- and mushroom-scented turf,
The slate-hung farms, the oil-lit chapels,
Thin elms and lemon-coloured apples –
Going and gone beyond recall

Now she is free for 'One and All'.

One day a tidal wave will break
Before the breakfasters awake
And sweep the cara's out to sea,
The oil, the tar, and you and me,
And leave in windy criss-cross motion
A waste of undulating ocean
With, jutting out, a second Scilly,
The isles of Roughtor and Brown Willy.

SIR JOHN BETJEMAN

'One and All': the motto of Cornwall
Roughtor: pronounced Rowtor, is the second highest peak in Cornwall; a
  near-neighbour to Brown Willy, and also on Bodmin Moor
Brown Willy: probably from the Cornish *bryn whella*, meaning 'highest
  hill', is the highest point in Cornwall

The poem's title here means the whole county of Cornwall. Strictly speaking, the Cornish Duchy consists of the estates owned by the Duke of Cornwall, eldest son of the reigning Sovereign. The Cornish author 'Q.' (Sir Arthur Quiller-Couch) called one of his books *The Delectable Duchy* (1893).

SUMMER BEACH

For how long known this boundless wash of light;
This smell of purity; this gleaming waste;
This wind? This brown, strewn wrack how old a sight,
These pebbles round to touch and salt to taste?

See, the slow, marbled heave, the liquid arch,
Before the waves' procession to the land
Flowers in foam; the ripples onward march;
Their last caresses on the pure hard sand.

For how long known these bleaching corks, new-made,
Smooth and enchanted from the lapping sea?
Since first I laboured with a wooden spade
Against the background of Eternity.

FRANCES CORNFORD

HARBOUR
AND ISLAND,
CAPE AND CLIFF

HARBOUR

a harbour with the
boats going in and out
at top speed their sirens
blowing and their funnels trailing
long smoke and the tousled
bluejackets of the waves emptying
their pockets to the wind's
hornpipe and far down
in the murky basements the turning
of bright bodies smooth
as a bell mermaids you
say but I say
fish

R. S. THOMAS

CHARLESTOWN HARBOUR

In the little port,
Where the ships come rarely now,
In the silence of the street
A thrush sings – you know how:

Causing the echoes to fall
Like flowers upon the quay,
Reaching over the water
To the deserted street and me,

Standing and looking down
Upon the little Dutch ship,
Her tattered flag at the mast
Fluttering by the slip.

85

While, at the harbour-mouth,
The wind-awakened sea
Thunders, besieges the pier,
Comes nostrilling over the quay;

And on the outer beach
With dark and sullen roar,
With regular lapse and beat
Breaks upon the shore.

Here in an inland town,
Three hundred miles away,
I hear the sound and taste
The salt rime on the spray:

See before my eye
Harbour-mouth and quay,
Hear the song of a bird,
The remembered surge of the sea.

A. L. ROWSE

Charlestown, where china clay is exported and Welsh coal imported, is on
St Austell Bay in South Cornwall. The 'inland town' is Oxford, where the
poem was written during the Second World War.

A CHANNEL RHYME

Start Point and Beachy Head
Tell their tale of quick and dead.

Forelands both and Dungeness
See many a ship in dire distress.

The Lizard and the Longships know
Oft the end of friend and foe.

And many and many a seaman's knell
Has been rung by Manacles bell.

Gull and Dodman ask aright
A wide berth on a dirty night.

Bolt Head and Bolt Tail
Are ill spots in a Channel gale.

Over nigh to Portland Bill
In Channel fog it's just as ill.

And Wolf Rock and Seven Stones
Rest their feet on sailors' bones.

But from Nore Light to Cape Cornwall
Goodwin Sands are worst of all!

C. FOX SMITH

FOGHORNS

When Catrin was a small child
She thought the foghorn moaning
Far out at sea was the sad
Solitary voice of the moon
Journeying to England.
She heard it warn 'Moon, Moon',
As it worked the Channel, trading
Weather like rags and bones.

Tonight, after the still sun
And the silent heat, as haze
Became rain and weighed glistening
In brimful leaves, and the last bus
Splashes and fades with a soft
Wave-sound, the foghorns moan, moon-
Lonely and the dry lawns drink.
This dimmed moon, calling still,
Hawls sea-rags through the streets.

GILLIAN CLARKE

SKERRYVORE: THE PARALLEL

Here all is sunny, and when the truant gull
Skims the green level of the lawn, his wing
Dispetals roses; here the house is framed
Of kneaded brick and the plumed mountain pine,
Such clay as artists fashion and such wood
As the tree-climbing urchin breaks. But there
Eternal granite hewn from the living isle
And dowelled with brute iron, rears a tower
That from its wet foundation to its crown
Of glittering glass, stands, in the sweep of winds,
Immovable, immortal, eminent.

ROBERT LOUIS STEVENSON

dowelled: fastened together

For generations, the Stevensons were a famous family of civil engineers, responsible for designing and building many Scottish lighthouses. That at Skerryvore (the name means 'great rock') was built in 1844 by R.L.S.'s uncle, Alan Stevenson (1807–1865).

SHIAN BAY

Gulls set the long shore printed
With arrow steps over this morning's
Sands clean of a man's footprint
And set up question and reply
Over the serpentine jetty
And over the early coaches
Of foam noisily in rows
Driven in from the farout banks.

Last gale washed five into the bay's stretched arms,
Four drowned men and a boy drowned into shelter.
The stones roll out to shelter in the sea.

W. S. GRAHAM

GIGHA

That firewood pale with salt and burning green
Outfloats its men who waved with a sound of drowning
Their saltcut hands over mazes of this rough bay.

Quietly this morning beside the subsided herds
Of water I walk. The children wade the shallows.
The sun with long legs wades into the sea.

W. S. GRAHAM

THE CHILD ON THE CLIFFS

Mother, the root of this little yellow flower
Among the stones has the taste of quinine.
Things are strange to-day on the cliff. The sun shines so
   bright,
And the grasshopper works at his sewing-machine
So hard. Here's one on my hand, mother, look;
I lie so still. There's one on your book.

But I have something to tell more strange. So leave
Your book to the grasshopper, mother dear, –
Like a green knight in a dazzling market-place, –
And listen now. Can you hear what I hear
Far out? Now and then the foam there curls
And stretches a white arm out like a girl's.

Fishes and gulls ring no bells. There cannot be
A chapel or church between here and Devon,
With fishes or gulls ringing its bell, – hark! –
Somewhere under the sea or up in heaven.
'It's the bell, my son, out in the bay
On the buoy. It does sound sweet today.'

Sweeter I never heard, mother, no, not in all Wales.
I should like to be lying under that foam,
Dead, but able to hear the sound of the bell,
And certain that you would often come
And rest, listening happily.
I should be happy if that could be.

EDWARD THOMAS

ON THIS ISLAND

Look, stranger, on this island now
The leaping light for your delight discovers,
Stand stable here
And silent be,
That through the channels of the ear
May wander like a river
The swaying sound of the sea.

Here at the small field's ending pause
When the chalk wall falls to the foam and its tall ledges
Oppose the pluck
And knock of the tide,
And the shingle scrambles after the suck-
-ing surf,
And the gull lodges
A moment on its sheer side.

Far off like floating seeds the ships
Diverge on urgent voluntary errands,
And the full view
Indeed may enter
And move in memory as now these clouds do,
That pass the harbour mirror
And all the summer through the water saunter.

W. H. AUDEN

THE LAND'S END

On the sea
The sunbeams tremble, and the purple light
Illumes the dark Bolerium, seat of storms.
High are his granite rocks; his frowning brow
Hangs o'er the smiling ocean. In his caves
The Atlantic breezes murmur; in his caves,
Where sleep the haggard spirits of the storm.
Wild, dreary are the frowning rocks around,
Encircled by the wave, where to the breeze
The haggard cormorant shrieks; and far beyond,
Where the great ocean mingles with the sky,
Are seen the cloud-like islands, grey in mist.

SIR HUMPHRY DAVY

Bolerium: also Bellerium; the old Roman name for the Land's End area of
Cornwall

As well as being a celebrated chemist, and one whose inventions included
the miner's safety-lamp, the Cornishman Sir Humphry Davy (1778–1829)
wrote much verse and prose, including a book on fly-fishing.

PORTO BELLO

The port is unsuspected from the east,
Slowly the bay draws open, with still water,
Deeper and deeper yet, to the calm pond,
Hot, stagnant, wrinkleless, of palest gray.

There is the city at the end at last,
The dirty, gray stone platform of the fort,
To left of what remains, a few small houses,
The little river and a scarlet barn.

Once all the bells in England rang with joy
That we had captured this; we have two poems,
A painting and commemorative pots
(Jugs and quart mugs) which celebrate the feat.

Two generations since, an English ship
Lay here surveying: one aboard her told me
That all her seamen were beset with boils
Like Egypt in the Book of Exodus;
Their chart is still the sailor's guidance here.

How many English bones lie underneath
That stirless water, Drake's men; Morgan's men;
The buccaneers; all Admiral Hosier's men;
The men with Vernon; christened in the fonts
Of English churches, and now welded white
With shells, or waving scarlet with soft tendrils,
Part of a sea-floor where no anchors fall
Nor any shadow of an English ship.

Near, in the blueness of the haze, an island
Rises before us as we pass the port;
It is Escudo, where Sir Francis Drake
'Yielded his valiant spirit like a Christian.'
Some say 'His heart is buried there': perhaps.
His body lies beneath us somewhere here.
The surf breaks on the island as we pass.

JOHN MASEFIELD

Porto Bello: a village on the Caribbean Sea, north-east of Colon, Panama

ABOVE THE DOCK

Above the quiet dock in midnight,
Tangled in the tall mast's corded height,
Hangs the moon. What seemed so far away
Is but a child's balloon, forgotten after play.

T. E. HULME

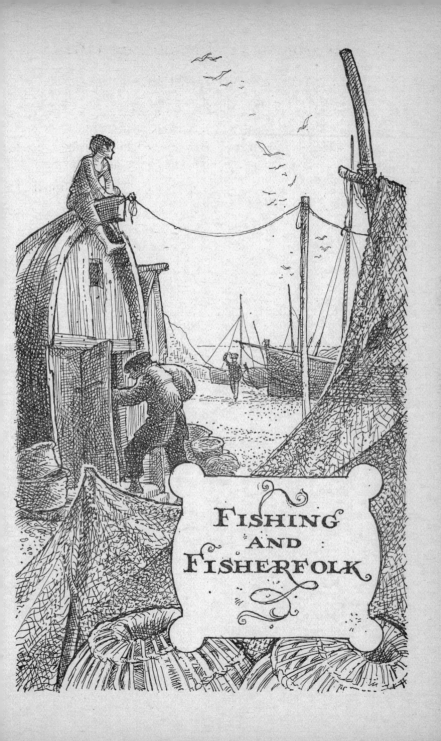

FISHING
AND
FISHERFOLK

FISHERMAN

The west flushed, drove down its shutter
And night sealed all.

Peaceful the air, the sea.
A quiet scattering of stars.

The great ocean
Makes the gentlest of motions about the turning world,
A thin wash through the pebbles.

No moon this night.
The creels lie still on their weeded ledges.

Not a sound, except far inland
The yelp of a tinker's dog.

Three days ago a storm blazed here, and drowned
Jock Halcrow among his lobsters.

There's one croft dark to-night in the lighted valley.

GEORGE MACKAY BROWN

UNCLE RODERICK

His drifter swung in the night
from a mile of nets
between the Shiants and Harris.

My boy's eyes watched
the lights of the fishing fleet – fireflies
on the green field of the sea.

In the fo'c'sle he gave me a bowl
of tea, black, strong and bitter,
and a biscuit you hammered
in bits like a plate.

The fiery curtain came up
from the blackness, comma'd with corpses.

Round Rhu nan Cuideagan
he steered for home, a boy's god
in seaboots. He found his anchorage
as a bird its nest.

In the kitchen he dropped
his oilskins where he stood.

He was strong as the red bull.
He moved like a dancer.
He was a cran of songs.

NORMAN MACCAIG

cran: a measure of fresh herrings (about 750 fish)

NOW TWO OLD SALTS, WHO KNEW THE FISHER'S TRADE

Now two old salts, who knew the fisher's trade,
Of dry sea-moss a lowly bed had made
Under a wattled hut, hard by a wall
Of leaves. Their tackle lay to hand withal,
Scattered about them: rods and creels of reeds,
And nets and hooks and lines all stiff with weeds,
And horsehair leaders, and full many a snare

For crayfish plaited, and a weathered pair
Of oars and cords all tangled in a maze,
And an old skiff drawn high upon the ways.
Under their heads were rolled thin cloaks of frieze;
Thick jackets were their coverlids; for these
Were all their substance and their property;
All else for them were superfluity.
Key, dog, or door they needed not for guard;
Over them Poverty kept watch and ward.
No neighbour near their cabin would abide,
Only the soft encroachment of the tide.

THEOCRITUS
From *Idyll* XXI
Translated from the Greek by H. H. Chamberlin

leaders: the end parts of reel-lines
frieze: coarse woollen cloth
coverlids: coverlets; top coverings of a bed

FISHING

We fish
in a sea worn smooth by last week's gales,
so flat and glassy
that if you breathed on it, it would mist.
There's no depth to it.
When I lean over the side
someone drops a weighted hook towards me.
Fish should come
through the hole he makes in my skull
but none do.
In the bottom of the boat
there lies just one small mackerel,

99

caught hours ago,
its colours dulled by its long immersion.

My father leans back on the oars;
a touch now and again is all he needs
to keep us stem-first to the tide.
His left hand knows what his right is doing.
'When I was young,' he says, 'it was worthwhile.'
He casts his mind back into the past
and fish after fish rises to the kill.
The deeper he goes the bigger they get.
When he was a boy
they were as tall almost as himself.
'It was before your time,' he says.
'It was before the trawlers came.'

Yes. I know about the trawlers.
I pretend to be examining my coat sleeve
but am really looking at my watch.
'There will be time,' it says, 'before your time,'
but when I breathe on it, it mists.
A catspaw dances across the water.
The Atlantic opens one eye, then goes back to sleep.

ALASDAIR MACLEAN

catspaw: a slight breeze, causing ripples on the sea's surface

I SIT UP HERE AT MIDNIGHT

I sit up here at midnight,
  The wind is in the street,
The rain besieges the windows
  Like the sound of many feet.

I see the street lamps flicker,
  I see them wink and fail,
The streets are wet and empty,
  It blows an easterly gale.

Some think of the fisher skipper
  Beyond the Inchcape stone;
But I of the fisher woman
  That lies at home alone.

She raises herself on her elbow
  And watches the firelit floor;
Her eyes are bright with terror,
  Her heart beats fast and sore.

Between the roar of the flurries,
  When the tempest holds his breath
She holds her breathing also –
  It is all as still as death.

She can hear the cinders dropping,
  The cat that purrs in its sleep –
The foolish fisher woman!
  Her heart is on the deep.

ROBERT LOUIS STEVENSON

MERRY SEAN LADS

With a cold north wind and a cockled sea,
   Or an autumn's cloudless day,
At the huer's bid, to stem we row,
   Or upon our paddles play.
All the signs, 'East, West, and Quiet,
   Could Roos,' too well we know;
We can bend a stop, secure a cross,
   For brave sean lads are we!
Chorus We can bend a stop, secure a cross,
   For brave sean lads are we!

If we have first stem when heva comes
   We'll the huer's bushes watch;
We will row right off or quiet lie,
   Flying summer sculls to catch.
And when he winds the towboat round,
   We will all ready be,
When he gives Could Roos, we'll shout hurrah!
   Merry sean lads are we!
Chorus When he gives Could Roos, we'll shout hurrah!
   Merry sean lads are we!

When the sean we've shot, upon the tow,
   We will heave with all our might,
With a heave! heave O! and rouse! rouse O!
   Till the huer cries, 'All right.'
Then on the bunt place kegs and weights,
   And next to tuck go we.
We'll dip, and trip, with a 'Hip hurrah!'
   Merry sean lads are we!

Chorus We'll dip, and trip, with a 'Hip hurrah!'
Merry sean lads are we!

C. TAYLOR STEPHENS

cockled sea: of little, tumbling waves
to stem: to wait at an appointed place ready to shoot a seine
sculls: shoals of fish
bunt: the bag of a net
tuck: to take the enclosed fish from the seine with a smaller net, the 'tuck-net'

' "Heva" is shouted from the hills, upon which a watch is kept for the approach of pilchards by the "huer", who telegraphs to the boats by means of bushes covered with white cloth, or, in modern days, with wire frames so covered. These signals are well understood, and the men in the seine and the other boats act according to the huer's directions. The . . . song contains all the terms employed in the fishing; many of them, especially *Could Roos*, do not appear to have any definite meaning attached to them . . . [although] *Could Roos*, or *Cold-ruse*, may . . . signify the original for '*shooting the seine*', or net; *roos* or *ruz* being the Cornish for net, or pilchard *seine*. . . The net is spelled sometimes *seine* at others *sean*.

'The song is by the late C. Taylor Stephens of St Ives, who was for some time the rural postman to Zennor. I employed Mr Taylor Stephens for some time collecting all that remains of legendary tales and superstitions in Zennor and Morva.'

From *Popular Romances of the West of England* collected and edited by Robert Hunt, F.R.S., 3rd edition, 1881.

THE FISHERMEN'S SONG

O blithely shines the bonnie sun
Upon the Isle of May,
And blithely rolls the morning tide
Into St Andrew's bay.

When haddocks leave the Firth of Forth,
And mussels leave the shore,
When oysters climb up Berwick Law,
We'll go to sea no more,
No more,
We'll go to sea no more.

ANONYMOUS

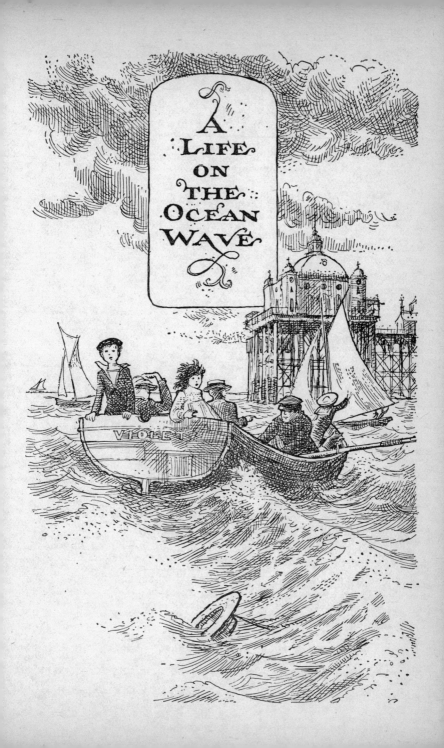
A LIFE ON THE OCEAN WAVE

JACK THE GUINEA-PIG

When the anchor's weigh'd and the ship's unmoored,
   And the landsmen lag behind sir,
The sailor joyful skips on board,
   And, swearing, prays for a wind, sir:
                Towing here,
                Yehoing there,
                Steadily, readily,
                Cheerily, merrily,
Still from care and thinking free,
Is a sailor's life, at sea.

When we sail with a fresh'ning breeze,
   And landsmen all grow sick, sir,
The sailor lolls, with his mind at ease,
   And the song and the can go quick, sir:
                Laughing here,
                Quaffing there,
                Steadily, etc.

When the wind at night whistles o'er the deep,
   And sings to landsmen dreary,
The sailor fearless goes to sleep,
   Or takes his watch most cheery:
                Boozing here,
                Snoozing there,
                Steadily, etc.

When the sky grows black and the wind blows hard
   And landsmen skulk below, sir,
Jack mounts up to the top sail yard,
   And turns his quid as he goes, sir:
                Hauling here,
                Bawling there,
                Steadily, etc.

When the foaming waves run mountains high,
    And landsmen cry 'All's gone', sir,
The sailor hangs 'twixt sea and sky,
    And he jokes with Davy Jones, sir!
            Dashing here,
            Clashing there,
            Steadily, etc.

When the ship, d'ye see, becomes a wreck,
    And landsmen hoist the boat, sir,
The sailor scorns to quit the deck,
    While a single plank's afloat, sir:
            Swearing here,
            Tearing there,
            Steadily, readily,
            Cheerily, merrily,
Still from care and thinking free,
Is a sailor's life, at sea.

                                    ANONYMOUS

guinea-pig: sea slang for a midshipman in the East Indian Service, *c.* 1750
turns his quid: chews tobacco; alters its position in the mouth

COME CHEER UP MY LADS

Come cheer up my lads, 'tis to glory we steer,
To add something new to this wonderful year;
To honour we call you, not press you like slaves,
For who are so free as the sons of the waves?

Heart of Oak are our ships, Heart of Oak are our men,
    We always are ready,
    Steady, boys, steady,
We'll fight and we'll conquer again and again.

We ne'er meet our foes but we wish them to stay,
They never see us but they wish us away;
If they run, why, we follow, and run them ashore,
For if they won't fight us, we cannot do more.
Heart of Oak, etc.

DAVID GARRICK

From *Heart of Oak*, a song from David Garrick's
pantomime *Harlequin's Invasion*, written and
performed in 1759 to celebrate the naval victories
over the French at Lagos and Quiberon Bay, and
the battle of Quebec.

YE MARINERS OF ENGLAND

Ye Mariners of England
  That guard our native seas!
Whose flag has braved a thousand years
  The battle and the breeze!
Your glorious standard launch again
  To match another foe;
And sweep through the deep,
  While the stormy winds do blow!
While the battle rages loud and long
  And the stormy winds do blow.

The spirits of your fathers
  Shall start from every wave –
For the deck it was their field of fame,
  And Ocean was their grave:

Where Blake and mighty Nelson fell
　Your manly hearts shall glow,
As ye sweep through the deep,
　While the stormy winds do blow!
While the battle rages loud and long
　And the stormy winds do blow.

Britannia needs no bulwarks,
　No towers along the steep;
Her march is o'er the mountain-waves,
　Her home is on the deep.
With thunders from her native oak
　She quells the floods below,
As they roar on the shore,
　When the stormy winds do blow!
When the battle rages loud and long
　And the stormy winds do blow.

The meteor flag of England
　Shall yet terrific burn;
Till danger's troubled night depart
　And the star of peace return.
Then, then, ye ocean-warriors!
　Our song and feast shall flow
To the fame of your name,
　When the storm has ceased to blow!
When the fiery fight is heard no more,
　And the storm has ceased to blow.

THOMAS CAMPBELL

Admirals Blake and Nelson (v. 2) both died at sea: Robert Blake as his
ship entered Plymouth Sound in 1657, and Nelson off Cape Trafalgar in
1805.

SHE IS FAR FROM THE LAND

Cables entangling her,
Shipspars for mangling her,
Ropes, sure of strangling her
Blocks over-dangling her;
Tiller to batter her,
Topmast to shatter her,
Tobacco to spatter her;
Boreas blustering,
Boatswain quite flustering,
Thunder-clouds mustering
To blast her with sulphur –
If the deep don't engulf her;
Sometimes fear's scrutiny
Pries out a mutiny,
Sniffs conflagration,
Or hints at starvation:–
All the sea-dangers,
Buccaneers, rangers,
Pirates and Salle-men,
Algerine galleymen,
Tornadoes and typhons,
And horrible syphons,
And submarine travels
Thro' roaring sea-navels,
Everything wrong enough,
Long-boat not long enough,
Vessel not strong enough;
Pitch marring frippery,
The deck very slippery,
And the cabin – built sloping,
The Captain a-toping,

And the mate a blasphemer,
That names his Redeemer,
With inward uneasiness;
The cook known by greasiness,
The victuals beslubber'd,
Her bed – in a cupboard;
Things of strange christening,
Snatched in her listening,
Blue lights and red lights
And mention of dead-lights,
And shrouds made a theme of,
Things horrid to dream of, –
And *buoys* in the water,
To fear all exhort her;
Her friend no Leander,
Herself no sea-gander,
And ne'er a cork jacket
On board of the packet!
The breeze still a-stiffening,
The trumpet quite deafening;
Thoughts of repentance,
And Doomsday and sentence;
Everything sinister,
Not a church minister, –
Pilot a blunderer,
Coral reefs under her,
Ready to sunder her;
Trunks tipsy-topsy,
The ship in a dropsy;
Waves oversurging her,
Sirens a-dirgeing her;
Sharks all expecting her,
Swordfish dissecting her,

Crabs with their hand-vices
Punishing land vices;
Sea-dogs and unicorns,
Things with no puny horns,
Mermen carnivorous –
'Good Lord deliver us!'

THOMAS HOOD

Boreas: the north-wind (Greek god)
Salle-men: pirate-ships (from Sallee, on the west coast of Morocco)
Algerine: Algerian
a-toping: drinking heavily
beslubber'd: spoilt; dealt with carelessly
Leander: a legendary youth who swam each night across the Hellespont (a
    distance of about 4 miles) to see Hero, the girl he loved
a-dirgeing: singing a funeral song

Thomas Moore (1779–1852), an Irish poet born twenty years earlier than
Hood, also wrote a poem called 'She is Far from the Land', in which a girl
laments the death of her lover:

'She is far from the land where her young hero sleeps,
    And lovers are round her, sighing:
But coldly she turns from their gaze, and weeps,
    For her heart in his grave is lying.'

The lines refer to Robert Emmett, who was executed in 1803 for his
involvement in the uprising of the United Irishmen, and Sarah Curran,
who although married eventually to another (an officer, who took her to
Italy) died of a broken heart.

Moore was also a musician, and many of his poems (like this one)
became famous songs.

HUZZA! HODGSON, WE ARE GOING

Huzza! Hodgson, we are going,
  Our embargo's off at last;
Favourable breezes blowing
  Bend the canvas o'er the mast.
From aloft the signal's streaming,
  Hark! the farewell gun is fired;
Women screeching, tars blaspheming,
  Tell us that our time's expired.
    Here's a rascal
    Come to task all,
  Prying from the custom-house,
    Trunks unpacking,
    Cases cracking,
  Not a corner for a mouse
'Scapes unsearch'd amid the racket
Ere we sail on board the Packet.

Now our boatmen quit their mooring,
  And all hands must ply the oar;
Baggage from the quay is lowering,
  We're impatient, push from shore.
'Have a care! that case holds liquor –
  Stop the boat – I'm sick – oh Lord!'
'Sick, ma'am, damme, you'll be sicker
  Ere you've been an hour on board.'
    Thus are screaming
    Men and women,
  Gemmen, ladies, servants, Jacks;
    Here entangling,
    All are wrangling,
  Stuck together close as wax. –

Such the general noise and racket,
Ere we reach the Lisbon Packet...

Now at length we're off for Turkey,
   Lord knows when we shall come back!
Breezes foul and tempests murky
   May unship us in a crack.
But, since life at most a jest is,
   As philosophers allow,
Still to laugh by far the best is,
   Then laugh on – as I do now.
     Laugh at all things,
     Great and small things,
Sick or well, at sea or shore;
     While we're quaffing,
     Let's have laughing –
Who the devil cares for more? –
Some good wine! and who would lack it,
Ev'n on board the Lisbon Packet?

GEORGE GORDON, LORD BYRON
From *Lines to Mr Hodgson*

Written on Board the Lisbon Packet (Falmouth Roads, 30 June 1809)

Byron had met the Rev. Francis Hodgson in 1807 at Cambridge, where
he was a tutor at King's College.

I CAN SING A TRUE SONG
ABOUT MYSELF

I can sing a true song about myself,
Tell of my travels, of many hard times
Toiling day after day; I can describe
How I have harboured bitter sorrow in my heart
And often learned that ships are homes of sadness.

115

Wild were the waves when I took my turn,
The arduous night-watch, standing at the prow
While the boat tossed near the rocks. My feet
Were tortured by frost, fettered
In frozen chains; fierce anguish clutched
At my heart; passionate longings maddened
The mind of the sea-weary man. Prosperous men,
Living on land, do not begin to understand
How I, careworn and cut off from my kinsmen,
Have as an exile endured the winter
On the icy sea . . .
Icicles hung round me; hail showers flew.
The only sound there, was of the sea booming –
The ice-cold wave – and at times the song of the swan.
The cry of the gannet was all my gladness,
The call of the curlew, not the laughter of men,
The mewing gull, not the sweetness of mead.
There, storms echoed off the rocky cliffs; the icy-
    feathered tern
Answered them; and often the eagle,
Dewy-winged, screeched overhead. No protector
Could console the cheerless man.

ANONYMOUS
From The Seafarer
Translated from the Anglo-Saxon by Kevin Crossley-Holland

Though the manuscript of *The Seafarer* was given, with others, to Exeter
Cathedral in about the year 1060, and is still in the Cathedral library there,
the tale it tells could be heard in any sea-port today. It is usually taken to
be a conversation between a young man who longs to go to sea, and an old
and experienced sailor who knows only too well that although the seaman's
lot can be harsh and bitter, there is really no other kind of life he would
wish to lead. Later on, the poem compares life on earth with heaven.

ABOARD AT A SHIP'S HELM

Aboard at a ship's helm,
A young steersman steering with care.

Through fog on a sea-coast dolefully ringing,
An ocean-bell – O a warning bell, rock'd by the waves.

O you give good notice indeed, you bell by the sea-
    reefs ringing,
Ringing, ringing, to warn the ship from its wreck-
    place.

For as on the alert, O steersman, you mind the loud
    admonition,
The bows turn, the freighted ship tacking speeds away
    under her grey sails,
The beautiful and noble ship with all her precious
    wealth speeds away gaily and safe.

But O the ship, the immortal ship! O ship aboard the
    ship!
Ship of the body, ship of the soul, voyaging, voyaging,
    voyaging.

WALT WHITMAN
From *Leaves of Grass*

RIDDLE

A curious, fair creature came floating on the waves,
shouting out to the distant shores,
resounding very loudly; her laughter was terrible
and fearsome to all. Sharp were her edges.
She is slow to join battle but severe in the fray,
smashing great ships with savagery.
She binds them with baleful charm,
and speaks with characteristic cunning:
'My mother, one of the beloved maidens,
is my daughter also, swollen and strong,
known by all people as she falls on the earth,
welcomed with love through the width of all lands.'

ANONYMOUS

Translated from the Anglo-Saxon by Kevin Crossley-Holland

Answer: iceberg; the mother of iceberg is water, and if the iceberg
melts again, the result – her 'child' – is water once more

VESSELS

THE ARK

Nobody knows just how they went.
They certainly went in two by two,
But who preceded the kangaroo
And who dared follow the elephant?

'I've had enough,' said Mrs Noah.
'The food just won't go round,' she said.
A delicate deer raised up his head
As if to say, '*I* want no more.'

In they marched and some were sick.
All very well for those who could be
On the rough or the calm or the middle sea.
But I must say that ark felt very thick

Of food and breath. How wonderful
When the dove appeared and rested upon
The hand of Noah. All fear was gone,
The sea withdrew, the air was cool.

ELIZABETH JENNINGS

'TWAS WHEN THE RAIN FELL STEADY

'Twas when the rain fell steady an' the Ark was pitched
    an' ready,
  That Noah got his orders for to take the bastes
    below;
He dragged them all together by the horn an' hide an'
    feather,
  An' all excipt the Donkey was agreeable to go.

First Noah spoke him fairly, thin talked to sevairely,
   An' thin he cursed him squarely to the glory av the
     Lord: –
'Divil take the ass that bred you, and the greater ass
   that fed you!
  'Divil go wid ye, ye spalpeen!' an' the Donkey wint
   aboard.

But the wind was always failin', an' 'twas most onaisy
   sailin',
  An' the ladies in the cabin couldn't stand the stable
   air;
An' the bastes betwuxt the hatches, they tuk an' died
   in batches,
  Till Noah said: – 'There's wan av us that hasn't
   paid his fare!'

For he heard a flusteration 'mid the bastes av all
   creation –
  The trumpetin' av elephints an' bellowin' av whales;
An' he saw forninst the windy whin he wint to stop the
   shindy
  The Divil wid a stable-fork bedivillin' their tails.

The Divil cursed outrageous, but Noah said
   umbrageous: –
  'To what am I indebted for this tenant-right
   invasion?'
An' the Divil gave for answer: 'Evict me if you can, sir,
  'For I came in wid the Donkey – on Your Honour's
   invitation!'

RUDYARD KIPLING
From *The Legends of Evil*

SAILING

Consider the Viking keel
Cutting keen,
Slicing over the green deep.

Hear the hiss of the salt foam
Curling off at the bow,
And the wake closing quietly
In bubbles behind.

Listen to the sound of the thumping drum,
See the helmets shine in the sun.
Feel, with your finger,
The full sail drawn tight
As they drive home before the wind.

DAVID ENGLISH

'TIN FISH'

The ships destroy us above
    And ensnare us beneath.
We arise, we lie down, and we move
    In the belly of Death.

The Ships have a thousand eyes
    To mark where we come. . .
But the mirth of a seaport dies
    When our blow gets home.

RUDYARD KIPLING

Tin Fish: here, a submarine; also naval slang for a torpedo

BOATS AND PLACES

1
row the sea
row it easy
Rothesay

2
Greek
      creek
creak
caïque

3
dhow
whoa
    Howrah
    hurrah
    howdah
       andhow

4
junk tug shag wee tow
bang two carp long catch
sam pan bet men go
oh ho
Hong Kong crow sing snatch

5
the Nore
an oar
no more

6
– rat-tat-tat!
– Ataturk?
– Van cat!
– caravan?
– catamaran!
– ark track?
– Ararat!

EDWIN MORGAN

FISHING BOATS IN MARTIGUES

Around the quays, kicked off in twos
The Four Winds dry their wooden shoes.

ROY CAMPBELL

H.M.S. HERO

Pale grey, her guns hooded, decks clear of all
    impediment,
Easily, between the swart tugs, she glides in the pale
    October sunshine:
It is Saturday afternoon, and the men are at football,
The wharves and the cobbled streets are silent by the
    slow river.

Smoothly, rounding the long bend, she glides to her
    place in history,
Past the grimed windows cracked and broken,
Past Swan Hunter's, Hawthorn Leslie's, Armstrong's,
Down to the North Sea, and trials, and her first
    commission.

Here is grace; and a job well done; built only for one end.
Women watch from the narrow doorways and give no
    sign,
Children stop playing by the wall and stare in silence
At gulls wheeling above the Tyne, or the ship passing.

MICHAEL ROBERTS

WITH SHIPS THE SEA WAS SPRINKLED FAR AND NIGH

With Ships the sea was sprinkled far and nigh,
Like stars in heaven, and joyously it showed;
Some lying fast at anchor in the road,
Some veering up and down, one knew not why.
A goodly Vessel did I then espy
Come like a giant from a haven broad;
And lustily along the bay she strode,
Her tackling rich, and of apparel high.
This Ship was nought to me, nor I to her,
Yet I pursued her with a Lover's look;
This Ship to all the rest did I prefer:
When will she turn, and whither? She will brook
No tarrying; where She comes the winds must stir;
On went She, and due north her journey took.

WILLIAM WORDSWORTH

SUNDAY MORNING

Sunday morning
                and the sun
                bawls
                with
                his big mouth
Yachts
                paper triangles
                of white and blue
                crowd the sloping bay
                appearing motionless
                as if stuck there
                by some infant thumb

                beneath a shouting sky

                upon a painted sea

WES MAGEE

RIDDLE

This world is adorned in various ways.
I saw a strange contraption, an experienced traveller,
grind against the gravel and move away screaming.
This strange creature could not see; it had no shoulders,
arms, or hands; on one foot this oddity
journeys most rapidly, far over
the rolling sea. It has many ribs,
and a mouth in its middle, most useful to men.
It carries food in plenty, yielding tribute to all people
year by year, enjoyed by rich
and enjoyed by poor. Tell me if you can,
O man of wise words, what this creature is.

ANONYMOUS
Translated from the Anglo-Saxon by Kevin Crossley-Holland

Answer: ship

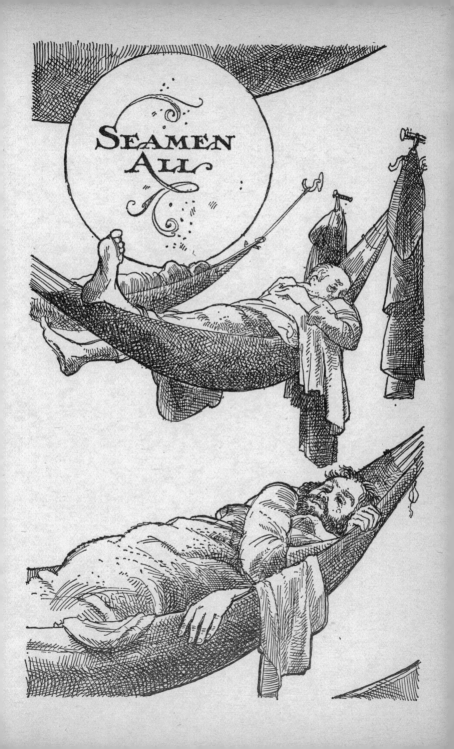

SEAMEN
ALL

ON A QUAY BY THE SEA

On a quay by the sea
with one hand on his knee
sat Skipper ('Double D.') Dhu,
resting his eyes on
the far horizon
for want of something to do.

Up and up like a cup
that can sip its own sup
rose the tides of the turbulent sea,
but gravely he sat
gazing over, not at,
the monsters that gnashed at his knee.

The whales lashed their tails
like terrible flails
and the shark clashed its portcullis jaw;
round and round by the jetty
like a lot of spaghetti
the octopus rose with a roar.

Dhu sits and he knits
his brows as befits
a Captain among such a welter;
then he lowers his eye
and all of them fly
down to Davy Jones' locker for shelter.

GEORGE BARKER

SEUMAS BEG

A man was sitting underneath a tree
Outside the village; and he asked me what
Name was upon this place; and said that he
Was never here before – He told a lot

Of stories to me too. His nose was flat!
I asked him how it happened, and he said
– The first mate of the Holy Ghost did that
With a marling-spike one day; but he was dead,

And jolly good job too; and he'd have gone
A long way to have killed him – Oh, he had
A gold ring in one ear; the other one
– 'Was bit off by a crocodile, bedad!' –

That's what he said. He taught me how to chew!
He was a real nice man! He liked me too!

JAMES STEPHENS

marling-spike: marline-spike; sharply-pointed iron tool for unravelling
the strands in rope in splicing (joining two ends of rope or cable
together)

FOLLOW THE SEA

'What is it makes a man follow the sea?
Ask me another!' says Billy Magee:
'Maybe it's liquor and maybe it's love –
Maybe it's likin' to be on the move –
Maybe the salt drop that runs in his blood
Won't let his killick lie snug in the mud:

What is it makes such poor idjits as me
Follow the sea – follow the sea? . . .
Jiggered if I know!' says Billy Magee.

'What is it keeps a chap rollin' around
All his life long from the Skaw to the Sound?
Samplin' the weathers from Hull to Rangoon –
Doldrums an' westerlies, Trade an' typhoon –
Hurricane, cyclone an' southerly buster –
In any old drogher as flies the Red Duster?
What is it makes a chap follow the sea –
Follow the sea – follow the sea –
Bust me if I know!' says Billy Magee.

'What is it makes a man stick to the sea?
Ah, you may ask me!' says Billy Magee.
'Stick to it hungry an' stick to it cold,
Stick to it after he's broken and old,
Freeze in the Forties an' sweat on the Line,
Shiver an' burn in the rain an' the shine,
Stick it until he can't stick it no more –
Curse it an' leave it for something ashore –
Chuck up his shore job an' follow the sea –
Stick to an' live by an' die by the sea –
Search me if I know!' says Billy Magee.

C. FOX SMITH

killick: small anchor; heavy stone used as an anchor
drogher: coastal vessel (pronounced 'dro-ger')

A SAINT OF CORNWALL

I don't know who Saint Mawes was, but he surely
  can't have been
A stiff old stone gazebo on a carved cathedral screen,
Or a holy-looking customer rigged out in blue and red
In a sunset-coloured window with a soup-plate round
  his head.
But he must have been a skipper who had sailed the
  salt seas round
(Or at least as many of 'em as had in his time been found),
And sung his song and kissed his girl and had his share
  of fun,
Till he took and got religion, when his sailing days
  were done.

He must have had a ruddy face, a grey beard neatly
  trimmed,
And eyes, with crow's feet round them, neither age
  nor use had dimmed,
And he'd lean there on the jetty with his glass up to
  his eye,
And look across the Carrick Roads, and watch the ships
  go by,
And yarn with his old cronies of the ships he used to
  know,
And shipmates that he sailed with many and many a
  year ago,
In the West of England tin-boats on the Tyre and
  Sidon run,
Before he got religion or his sailing days were done.

And when he came at last to die, they'd lay him down
  to rest

On a green and grassy foreland sloping gently to the
    west,
Where the wind's cry and the gull's cry would be near
    him night and day,
And a rousing deep-sea shanty might come to him
    where he lay.
And they left him there a-sleeping, for to smell the
    harbour smells,
And to count the passing watches by the striking of the
    bells,
And listen to the sailormen a-singing in the sun,
Like a good old master mariner whose sailing days are
    done.

C. FOX SMITH

'*the Tyre and Sidon run*': traders from these Phoenician cities, in the
    eastern Mediterranean, are said to have come to Cornwall in ancient
    times in search of tin

The town of St Mawes lies opposite the port of Falmouth in Cornwall.
Carrick Roads (or Roadstead) is the estuary of the River Fal.

THE FINE PACIFIC ISLANDS

The jolly English Yellowboy
    Is a 'ansome coin when new,
The Yankee Double-eagle
    Is large enough for two.
O, these may do for seaport towns,
    For cities these may do;
But the dibbs that takes the Hislands
    Are the dollars of Peru:
      O, the fine Pacific Hislands,
      O, the dollars of Peru!

It's there we buy the cocoanuts
    Mast 'eaded in the blue;
It's there we trap the lasses
    All waiting for the crew;
It's there we buy the trader's rum
    What bores a seaman through . . .
In the fine Pacific Hislands
    With the dollars of Peru:
    In the fine Pacific Hislands
    With the dollars of Peru!

Now, messmates, when my watch is up,
    And I am quite broached to,
I'll give a tip to 'Evving
    Of the 'ansome thing to do:
Let 'em just refit this sailor-man
    And launch him off anew
To cruise among the Hislands
    With the dollars of Peru:
    In the fine Pacific Hislands
    With the dollars of Peru!

ROBERT LOUIS STEVENSON

yellowboy: gold coin, either a sovereign or a guinea
double-eagle: U.S. gold coin, bearing the image of the spread-eagle
    (emblem of the U.S.A.), valued at twenty dollars
when my watch is up: when my life is ended

THERE WAS A SKIPPER HAILING
FROM FAR WEST

There was a Skipper hailing from far west;
He came from Dartmouth, so I understood.
He rode a farmer's horse as best he could,
In a woollen gown that reached his knee.
A dagger on a lanyard falling free
Hung from his neck under his arm and down.
The summer heat had tanned his colour brown,
And certainly he was an excellent fellow.
Many a draught of vintage, red and yellow,
He'd drawn at Bordeaux, while the trader snored.
The nicer rules of conscience he ignored.
If, when he fought, the enemy vessel sank,
He sent his prisoners home; they walked the plank.
As for his skill in reckoning his tides,
Currents and many another risk besides,
Moons, harbours, pilots, he had such dispatch
That none from Hull to Carthage was his match.
Hardy he was, prudent in undertaking;
His beard in many a tempest had its shaking,
And he knew all the havens as they were
From Gottland to the Cape of Finisterre,
And every creek in Brittany and Spain;
The barge he owned was called *The Maudelayne.*

GEOFFREY CHAUCER
Translated into modern English by Nevill Coghill

THE QUEEN'S SPEECH

Gallants all of British blood,
Why do not ye saile on th' ocean flood?
I protest ye are not all worth a philberd,
Compared with Sir Humphry Gilberd.

THE QUEEN'S REASON

For he walkt forth in a rainy day;
To the New-found-land he took his way
With many a gallant fresh and green:
He never came home again. God bless the Queen.

ANONYMOUS
part of *Sir Francis Drake and Queen Elizabeth*
From *Wit and Drollery*, 1656

---

philberd: the nut of the cultivated hazel; filbert or St Philibert's nut, so called because it ripens by about his feast-day (22 August)

Sir Humphrey Gilbert (*c.* 1539–83) founded the first British colony in North America, Newfoundland, in 1583 in the name of Queen Elizabeth I. He was lost, with his whole crew, in the tiny vessel *Squirrel* (10 tons burden) off the Azores on the return voyage to England. His last words were, 'We are as near to heaven by sea as on land'.

DRAKE'S DRUM

Drake he's in his hammock an' a thousand mile away,
  (Capten, art tha sleepin' there below?),
Slung atween the round shot in Nombre Dios Bay,
  An' dreamin' arl the time o' Plymouth Hoe.
Yarnder lumes the Island, yarnder lie the ships,
  Wi' sailor lads a dancin' heel-an'-toe,
An' the shore-lights flashin', an' the night-tide dashin',
  He sees et arl so plainly as he saw et long ago.

Drake he was a Devon man, an' rüled the Devon seas,
  (Capten, art tha sleepin' there below?),
Rovin' tho' his death fell, he went wi' heart at ease,
  An' dreamin' arl the time o' Plymouth Hoe.
"Take my drum to England, hang et by the shore,
  Strike et when your powder's runnin' low;
If the Dons sight Devon, I'll quit the port o' Heaven,
  An' drum them up the Channel as we drummed them
    long ago."

Drake he's in his hammock till the great Armadas come,
  (Capten, art tha sleepin' there below?),
Slung atween the round shot, listenin' for the drum,
  An' dreamin' arl the time o' Plymouth Hoe.
Call him on the deep sea, call him up the Sound,
  Call him when ye sail to meet the foe;
Where the old trade's plyin' an' the old flag flyin'
  They shall find him ware an' wakin', as they found
    him long ago!

SIR HENRY NEWBOLT

HERE'S TO NELSON'S MEMORY!

Here's to Nelson's memory!
'Tis the second time that I, at sea,
Right off Cape Trafalgar here,
Have drunk it deep in British Beer.
Nelson for ever – any time
Am I his to command in prose or rhyme!
Give me of Nelson only a touch,
And I save it, be it little or much:
Here's one our Captain gives, and so
Down at the word, by George, shall it go!
He says that at Greenwich they point the beholder
To Nelson's coat, 'still with tar on the shoulder:
'For he used to lean with one shoulder digging,
'Jigging, as it were, and zig-zag-zigging
'Up against the mizen-rigging!'

ROBERT BROWNING
From *Nationality in Drinks*

THE SUB-MARINE

It was a brave and jolly wight,
    His cheek was baked and brown,
For he had been in many climes
    With captains of renown,
And fought with those who fought so well
    At Nile and Camperdown.

His coat it was a soldier coat,
    Of red with yellow faced,
But (merman-like) he looked marine

All downward from the waist;
His trousers were so wide and blue,
  And quite in sailor taste!

He put the rummer to his lips,
  And drank a jolly draught;
He raised the rummer many times –
  And ever as he quaffed,
The more he drank, the more the Ship
  Seemed pitching fore and aft!

The Ship seemed pitching fore and aft,
  As in a heavy squall;
It gave a lurch and down he went,
  Head-foremost in his fall!
Three times he did not rise, alas!
  He never rose at all!

But down he went, right down at once
  Like any stone he dived,
He could not see, or hear, or feel –
  Of senses all deprived!
At last he gave a look around
  To see where he arrived!

And all that he could see was green,
  Sea-green on every hand!
And then he tried to sound beneath,
  And all he felt was sand!
There he was fain to lie, for he
  Could neither sit nor stand!

And lo! above his head there bent
  A strange and staring lass!
One hand was in her yellow hair,

The other held a glass;
A mermaid she must surely be
    If ever mermaid was!

Her fish-like mouth was open wide,
    Her eyes were blue and pale,
Her dress was of the ocean green,
    When ruffled by a gale;
Thought he, 'Beneath that petticoat
    She hides a salmon-tail!'

She looked as siren ought to look,
    A sharp and bitter shrew,
To sing deceiving lullabies
    For mariners to rue, –
But when he saw her lips apart,
    It chilled him through and through!

With either hand he stopped his ears
    Against her evil cry;
Alas, alas, for all his care,
    His doom it seemed to die,
Her voice went ringing through his head,
    It was so sharp and high!

He thrust his fingers further in
    At each unwilling ear,
But still, in very spite of all,
    The words were plain and clear;
'I can't stand here the whole day long,
    To hold your glass of beer!'

With opened mouth and opened eyes,
    Up rose the Sub-marine,

And gave a stare to find the sands
    And deeps where he had been:
There was no siren with her glass!
    No waters ocean-green!

The wet deception from his eyes
    Kept fading more and more,
He only saw the barmaid stand
    With pouting lip before –
The small green parlour of The Ship,
    And little sanded floor!

THOMAS HOOD

Nile: Naval battle (1798) at Aboukir Bay, near Alexandria, in which a
   French fleet was defeated by the British under Nelson, 'the hero of the
   Nile'
Camperdown: village on the coast of north Holland, off which there was a
   British naval victory over the Dutch in 1797

TOM BOWLING

Here, a sheer hulk, lies poor Tom Bowling,
    The darling of our crew;
No more he'll hear the tempest howling,
    For Death has broached him to.
His form was of the manliest beauty,
    His heart was kind and soft;
Faithful below, he did his duty,
    But now he's gone aloft.

Tom never from his word departed,
    His virtues were so rare;
His friends were many and truehearted,
    His Poll was kind and fair.

143

And then he'd sing so blithe and jolly;
    Ah, many's the time and oft!
But mirth is turned to melancholy,
    For Tom is gone aloft.

Yet shall poor Tom find pleasant weather,
    When He, who all commands,
Shall give, to call Life's crew together,
    The word to pipe all hands.
Thus Death, who Kings and Tars despatches,
    In vain Tom's life has doffed.
For though his body's under hatches,
    His soul is gone aloft.

CHARLES DIBDIN

broach to: to cause a ship to veer or change course; to turn its head away
    from the wind and present its side to the waves
pipe all hands: an order, preceded by the sound of the boatswain's pipe or
    whistle, affecting the whole crew; to call the crew together; here also
    means 'resurrection day'
under hatches: below decks

The 'Tom' in the words of the song is thought to be the poet's brother,
Captain Thomas Dibdin, who died in Capetown in 1780 on the way home
from India. Originally, Tom Bowling was a character in *The Adventures
of Roderick Random* (1748) by Tobias Smollett, a novelist who was at one
time a surgeon's mate in the 18th-century navy.

THE PRESS-GANG

Here's the tender coming,
　　Pressing all the men;
　　　O, dear honey,
　　What shall we do then?
Here's the tender coming,
　　Off at Shields Bar.
Here's the tender coming,
　　Full of men of war.

Here's the tender coming,
　　Stealing of my dear;
　　　O, dear honey,
　　They'll ship you out of here,
They'll ship you foreign,
　　For that is what it means.
Here's the tender coming,
　　Full of red marines.

ANONYMOUS

tender: a boat in attendance upon a man-of-war
red marines: also known as 'lobster soldiers'; members of a corps first
　raised for sea service by King Charles II in 1664; a Royal Marine Light
　Infantryman of the time wore an orange-red uniform

PRESS-GANG

A man-of-war enchanted
Three boys away.
Pinleg, Windbag, Lord Rum returned.

GEORGE MACKAY BROWN

STORMALONG

O Stormy, he is dead and gone;
To my way you Stormalong.
O Stormy was a good old man;
Ay, ay, ay, Mister Stormalong.

We'll dig his grave with a silver spade,
And lower him down with a golden chain.

I wish I was old Stormy's son,
I'd build a ship of a thousand ton.

I'd fill her with New England rum,
And all my shell-backs they'd have some.

O Stormy's dead and gone to rest,
To my way you Stormalong.
Of all the sailors he was the best.
Ay, ay, ay, Mister Stormalong.

ANONYMOUS

shell-backs: tough and experienced old seamen

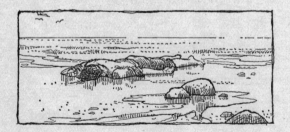

CAPTAIN LEAN

Out of the East a hurricane
   Swept down on Captain Lean –
That mariner and gentleman
   Will not again be seen.

He sailed his ship against the foes
   Of his own country dear,
But now in the trough of the billows
   An aimless course doth steer.

Powder was violets to his nostrils,
   Sweet the din of the fighting-line,
Now he is flotsam on the seas,
   And his bones are bleached with brine.

The stars move up along the sky,
   The moon she shines so bright,
And in that solitude the foam
   Sparkles unearthly white.

This is the tomb of Captain Lean,
   Would a straiter please his soul?
I trow he sleeps in peace,
   Howsoever the billows roll!

WALTER DE LA MARE

MESSMATES

He gave us all a good-bye cheerily
  At the first dawn of day;
We dropped him down the side full drearily
  When the light died away.
It's a dead dark watch that he's a-keeping there,
And a long, long night that lags a-creeping there,
Where the Trades and the tides roll over him
  And the great ships go by.

He's there alone with green seas rocking him
  For a thousand miles round;
He's there alone with dumb things mocking him,
  And we're homeward bound.
It's a long, lone watch that he's a-keeping there,
And a dead cold night that lags a-creeping there,
While the months and the years roll over him
  And the great ships go by.

I wonder if the tramps come near enough
  As they thrash to and fro,
And the battle-ships' bells ring clear enough
  To be heard down below;
If through all the lone watch that he's a-keeping there,
And the long, cold night that lags a-creeping there,
The voices of the sailor-men shall comfort him
  When the great ships go by.

SIR HENRY NEWBOLT

Messmates: a ship's company is divided into groups, each called a mess;
  messmates are those with whom a sailor eats and shares living-quarters
  when he is off-duty
dropped him down the side: the particularly sad and desolating occasion of
  a burial at sea

IF MY VOICE SHOULD DIE ON LAND

If my voice should die on land,
take it to sea-level
and leave it on the shore.

Take it to sea-level
and make it captain
of a white ship of war.

Oh my voice adorned
with naval insignia:
on the heart an anchor,
and on the anchor a star,
and on the star the wind,
and on the wind the sail!

RAFAEL ALBERTI
Translated from the Spanish by Mark Strand

THE FIRST LORD'S SONG

When I was a lad I served a term
As office boy to an Attorney's firm.
I cleaned the windows and I swept the floor,
And I polished up the handle of the big front door.
  I polished up the handle so successfullee
    That now I am the Ruler of the Queen's Navee!

As office boy I made such a mark
That they gave me the post of a junior clerk,
I served the writs with a smile so bland,
And I copied all the letters in a big round hand.
  I copied all the letters in a hand so free,
    That now I am the Ruler of the Queen's Navee!

In serving writs I made such a name
That an articled clerk I soon became;
I wore clean collars and a brand-new suit
For the Pass Examination at the Institute:
   And that Pass Examination did so well for me,
   That now I am the Ruler of the Queen's Navee!

Of legal knowledge I acquired such a grip
That they took me into the partnership,
And that junior partnership I ween,
Was the only ship that I ever had seen:
   But that kind of ship so suited me,
   That now I am the Ruler of the Queen's Navee!

I grew so rich that I was sent
By a pocket borough into Parliament;
I always voted at my Party's call,
And I never thought of thinking for myself at all.
   I thought so little, they rewarded me,
   By making me the Ruler of the Queen's Navee!

Now, landsmen all, whoever you may be,
If you want to rise to the top of the tree –
If your soul isn't fettered to an office stool,
Be careful to be guided by this golden rule –
   Stick close to your desks and never go to sea,
   And you all may be Rulers of the Queen's Navee!

W. S. GILBERT
From *H.M.S. Pinafore*

pocket borough: town in which the power to elect its Member of Parliament was under the control of a private person or family

THE DEATH OF PARKER

Ye gods above, protect the widows and with pity look
    down on me,
Help me, help me out of trouble and through this sad
    calamity.
Parker was a wild young sailor, fortune to him did
    prove unkind,
Although he was hanged up for mutiny, worse than
    him was left behind.

Chorus   Saying Farewell Parker, thou bright angel,
           Once thou wast old England's pride
           Although he was hanged up for mutiny
           Worse than him was left behind.

At length I see the yellow flag flying, the signal for my
    true love to die.
The gun was fired which was required to hang him all
    on the yard-arm so high.
The boatman did his best endeavour to reach the shore
    without delay
And there we stood waiting just as a marmot to carry
    the corpse of poor Parker away.

In the dead of night when all was silent thousands of
    people lay fast asleep,
Me and my poor maidens beside me sorrowfully into
    the burying-ground creep,
With trembling hands instead of shovels the mould
    from his coffin we scratched away
Until we came to the corpse of Parker and carried him
    home without delay.

A mourning-coach stood there a-waiting and off to
   London we drove with speed
And then we had him most decently buried, a funeral
   to him was preached indeed.

ANONYMOUS

Richard Parker, born in Exeter, Devon in about 1767, was the seaman
who led the famous mutiny at the Nore. The 'Floating Republic', which
included thirteen ships of the line, blockaded the River Thames and
refused to put to sea unless certain grievances were put right. The Naval
authorities crushed the mutiny, and on 30 June 1797 Parker was hanged
at the yard-arm.

Ballads were passed originally from one singer to another by word of
mouth. As a *marmot* (v. 2) is a burrowing rodent of the squirrel family, it
is possible that this is a mis-hearing of the word 'mermaid'.

THE CHANGELINGS
(R.N.V.R.)

Or ever the battered liners sank
   With their passengers to the dark,
I was head of a Walworth Bank,
   And you were a grocer's clerk.

I was a dealer in stocks and shares,
   And you in butters and teas;
And we both abandoned our own affairs
   And took to the dreadful seas.

Wet and worry about our ways –
   Panic, onset, and flight –
Had us in charge for a thousand days
   And a thousand-year-long night.

We saw more than the nights could hide –
   More than the waves could keep –
And – certain faces over the side
   Which do not go from our sleep.

We were more tired than words can tell
   While the pied craft fled by,
And the swinging mounds of the Western swell
   Hoisted us Heavens-high. . .

Now there is nothing – not even our rank –
   To witness what we have been;
And I am returned to my Walworth Bank,
   And you to your margarine!

RUDYARD KIPLING

R.N.V.R.: Royal Naval Volunteer Reserve

OFF BRIGHTON PIER

I saw him, a squat man with red hair,
Grown into sideburns, fishing off Brighton pier:
Suddenly he bent, and in a lumpy bag
Rummaged for bait, letting his line dangle,
And I noticed the stiffness of his leg
That thrust out, like a tripod, at an angle.
Then I remembered: the sideburns, that gloss
Of slicked-down ginger on a skin like candy floss.
He was there, not having moved, as last,
On a windless night, leaning against the mast,
I saw him, groping a bag for numbers.
And the date was the 17th of September,

15 years back, and we were playing Tombola
During the last Dog, someone beginning to holler
'Here you are' for a full card, and I remember
He'd just called 'Seven and six, she was worth it,'
When – without contacts or warning – we were hit.
Some got away with it, a few bought it.
And I recall now, when they carried him ashore,
Fishing gear lashed to his hammock, wishing
Him luck, and his faint smile, more
To himself than to me, when he saluted
From the stretcher, and, cadging a fag,
Cracked 'I'm quids in, it's only one leg,
They'll pension me off to go fishing.'

ALAN ROSS

last Dog: Second Dog Watch, from 6 p.m.–8 p.m.
quids in: in great good luck; a quid was slang for a golden sovereign
   or a guinea, as it is today for a pound

NAVAL PROMOTION

The Cabin Boy's over the sea,
For his sisters and mother weeps he;
Till good conduct prevails, and homeward he sails,
To land his full pockets with glee.

Next a Middy away o'er the wave,
'Tis his fortune in action to save
His officer's life, in the heat of the strife,
And he lands at home happy and brave.

Now an Officer over the main,
Fresh laurels on ocean to gain,
Till commanding a prize his friends see him rise,
And a Captain's commission obtain.

The Captain adventures once more,
Returning a bold Commodore!
And, his wishes to crown, he comes up to town
With an Admiral's flag at the fore.

THOMAS DIBDIN

Middy: midshipman, originally one stationed amidships, became a naval
rank in the British Navy after the Napoleonic wars: a junior officer
between a cadet and a sub-lieutenant; in the U.S. Navy, an ensign

HAS ANYBODY SEEN OUR SHIP?

Verse: What shall we do with the Drunken Sailor?
So the saying goes.
We're not tight but we're none too bright,
Great Scott! I don't suppose.
We've lost our way and we've lost our pay and to
make the thing complete
We've been and gone and lost the blooming fleet.

Refrain: Has anybody seen our Ship, the H.M.S.
'Peculiar'?
We've been on shore for a month or more
And when we see the captain we shall get what for.
Heave Ho! me Hearties, Sing Glory Hallelujah.
A lady bold as she could be
Pinched our whistles at the 'Golden Key'
Now we're in between the devil and the deep blue
sea.
Has anybody seen our ship?
Has anybody seen our ship?

SIR NOËL COWARD
From *Red Peppers*

Noël Coward also wrote the music for the one-act play from which this is taken.

IN DEEP

WATERFRONT BALLAD

Some say it isn't deep
But it's deep enough for me.
Don't write no address on my grave
But the Mediterranean Sea.

I shan't drift in to shore:
For they'll pickle me a treat.
And I shall walk in a tidy rig
Past the ships of many a fleet.

Ships you never heard of,
Fleets that went down in thunder:
And them old shipmates from all the wars
Sharing the Mediterranean plunder.

JOHN PUDNEY

LAMENT FOR A SAILOR

Here, where the night is clear as sea-water
And stones are white and the sticks are spars,
Swims on a windless, mackerel tide
The dolphin moon in a shoal of stars.

Here, in the limbo, where moths are spinners
And clouds like hulls drift overhead,
Move we must for our colder comfort,
I the living and you the dead.

Each on our way, my ghost, my grayling,
You to the water, the land for me;
I am the fat-knuckled, noisy diver
But you are the quietest fish in the sea.

PAUL DEHN

spinners: flies (or imitations) used as bait in fishing

METHOUGHT I SAW A THOUSAND FEARFUL WRACKS

CLARENCE Methought I saw a thousand fearful wracks;
  A thousand men that fishes gnawed upon;
  Wedges of gold, great anchors, heaps of pearl,
  Inestimable stones, unvalued jewels,
  All scattered in the bottom of the sea.
  Some lay in dead men's skulls; and in those holes
  Where eyes did once inhabit, there were crept
  (As 'twere in scorn of eyes) reflecting gems,
  That wooed the slimy bottom of the deep,
  And mocked the dead bones that lay scattered by.

WILLIAM SHAKESPEARE
From *King Richard III*

wracks: shipwrecks

IN MEMORY OF THE CIRCUS SHIP *EUZKERA*

The most stupendous show they ever gave
Must have been that *bizarrerie* of wreck;
The lion tamer spoke from a green wave
And lions slithered slowly off the deck.

Amazing! And the high-wire artists fell
(As we'd all hoped, in secret) through no net
And ten miles down, a plunge they must know well,
And landed soft, and there they're lying yet.

Then while the brass band played a languid waltz,
The elephant, in pearls and amethysts,
Toppled and turned his ponderous somersaults,
Dismaying some remote geologists.

The tiger followed, and the tiger's mate.
The seals leaped joyful from their brackish tank.
The fortune teller read the palm of Fate –
Beware of ocean voyages – and sank.

Full fathom five the fattest lady lies,
Among the popcorn and the caged baboons,
And dreams of mermaids' elegant surprise
To see the bunting and the blue balloons.

WALKER GIBSON

bizarrerie: something extremely odd; grotesque; eccentric

The *Euzkera* was wrecked in the Caribbean Sea in September 1948.

'Full fathom five thy father lies' is part of a song sung by the magic spirit,
Ariel, to Ferdinand, son of the King of Naples, in Shakespeare's play *The
Tempest*. Ferdinand believes himself to be the only survivor of a wreck in
which all the other passengers, including his father, were drowned.

POSTED AS MISSING

Dream after dream I see the wrecks that lie
Unknown of man, unmarked upon the charts,
Known of the flat-fish with the withered eye,
And seen by women in their aching hearts.

World-wide the scattering is of those fair ships
That trod the billow tops till out of sight:
The cuttle mumbles them with horny lips,
The shells of the sea-insects crust them white.

In silence and in dimness and in greenness
Among the indistinct and leathery leaves
Of fruitless life they lie among the cleanness.
Fish glide and flit, slow under-movement heaves:

But no sound penetrates, not even the lunge
Of live ships passing, nor the gannet's plunge.

JOHN MASEFIELD

THE WORLD BELOW THE BRINE

The world below the brine,
Forests at the bottom of the sea, the branches and
    leaves,
Sea-lettuce, vast lichens, strange flowers and seeds, the
    thick tangle, openings, and pink turf,
Different colours, pale grey and green, purple, white,
    and gold, the play of light through the water,
Dumb swimmers there among the rocks, coral, gluten,
    grass, rushes, and the aliment of the swimmers,
Sluggish existences grazing there suspended, or slowly
    crawling close to the bottom,
The sperm-whale at the surface blowing air and spray,
    or disporting with his flukes,
The leaden-eyed shark, the walrus, the turtle, the
    hairy sea-leopard, and the sting-ray,
Passions there, wars, pursuits, tribes, sight in those
    ocean-depths, breathing that thick-breathing air, as
    so many do,
The change thence to the sight here, and to the subtle
    air breathed by beings like us who walk this sphere,
The change onward from ours to that of beings who
    walk other spheres.

WALT WHITMAN
From *Leaves of Grass*

gluten: sticky substance
aliment: food

JONAH

A cream of phosphorescent light
Floats on the wash that to and fro
Slides round his feet – enough to show
Many a pendulous stalactite
Of naked mucus, whorls and wreaths
And huge festoons of mottled tripes
And smaller palpitating pipes
Through which a yeasty liquor seethes.

Seated upon the convex mound
Of one vast kidney, Jonah prays
And sings his canticles and hymns,
Making the hollow vault resound
God's goodness and mysterious ways,
Till the great fish spouts music as he swims.

ALDOUS HUXLEY

For the story of the Hebrew prophet Jonah, see the Old Testament Book
bearing his name.

FATHER MAPPLE'S HYMN

The ribs and terrors in the whale,
　Arched over me a dismal gloom,
While all God's sun-lit waves rolled by,
　And lift me deepening down to doom.

I saw the opening maw of hell,
　With endless pains and sorrows there;　·
Which none but they that feel can tell –
　Oh, I was plunging to despair.

In black distress, I called my God,
    When I could scarce believe him mine,
He bowed his ear to my complaints –
    No more the whale did me confine.

With speed he flew to my relief,
    As on a radiant dolphin borne;
Awful, yet bright, as lightning shone
    The face of my Deliverer God.

My song for ever shall record
    That terrible, that joyful hour;
I give the glory to my God,
    His all the mercy and the power.

HERMAN MELVILLE
From *Moby Dick*

The American writer Herman Melville went to sea as a cabin-boy, later
served in a whaler, and also in the South Seas, where he jumped ship and
lived for a time among cannibals. His novel *Moby Dick* (1851) tells the
story of the great white whale of that name, and its hunt by Captain Ahab
in the ship *Pequod*.

SEA-SIGNS

From the cliff-top
I watch a sailboat
Like a whip of wind
A white fleck in a fingernail of blue.

I have a photograph:
I fish off shallow rocks
With a long bamboo.
Waves clash
Spray dots my picture.
In summer I am surrounded by flecks of snow.

Melon seeds and Coca-Cola cans
Black olives like goat droppings
Collect on the water.
The sea has spread a blue tablecloth
And is having its picnic.

My face is caught in the water.
A small fish wriggles in my eye.

I dive from a caïque
And meet myself
On the sea's skin.

The sea closes my mouth
It likes quiet.
I must not shout
I am a guest under its roof.

The fisherman on his boat
Peers into the sea.
I smile, half-asleep
Looking up at him.
Slowly rising
My lips touch his cheek.

Underneath
My flippers brush the reef surface.
My eyes reach the reef's shelf
And fall out of my head.

My spear misses the inkfish.
Cut
My feet leak
A wake of red smoke.
From behind its black cloud
The inkfish skids closer.

Under the stained glass surface
Sunlight falls in shafts.
Spread-eagled in this cathedral
I fly over valleys
In spring bloom.

On the sea's marriage bed
Glowing fish thread themselves
Into veils of bright beads;
I kneel in pillows of sand
And they weave a groom's jewels around my head.

The sea has entered my blood
Its minerals live in my bones.
My tears are the salt sea in my eyes
My sweat is the salt sea on my skin.
On the sand's heat
Oceans break from me
I hear my fathers sing
Like Sirens.

GEORGE TARDIOS

THE DIVER

The blue-cold spasm passes,
And he's broken in.
Assailed by silence he descends
Lost suddenly

To air and sunburned friends,
And wholly underwater now
He plies his strength against
The element that

Slows all probings to their feint.
Still down, till losing
Light he drifts to the wealthy wreck
And its shade-mariners

Who flit about a fractured deck
That holds old purposes
In darkness. He hesitates, then
Wreathes his body in.

DICK DAVIS

CAER ARIANRHOD

A village in the sea! The map says that
Tradition says so, barely casting doubt
On the gaze and gossip of those generations
For whom a map could never end at the shore
Where livelihood begins, that salt harvest
To be shared with busts of seals who come to dine
Alone, like emperors, in the black waves.
Or with ghosts that the sea claimed from time to time
As at low tide upon a summer's night
A homeward boy tugging his skiff across
The calmed surface saw lights and shapes down there
Like faces of strangers in doorways looking out
Through unremembered evenings, and not a cry
To break the silence of the flood but the small
Pirate clink of the rowlocks at the pull of the oars
And the boat's terrified speed over the roof of the sea.

JOHN FULLER

RIDDLE

I must fight with the waves whipped up by the wind,
contending alone with their force combined,
when I dive to earth under the sea.
My own country is unknown to me.
If I can stay still, I'm strong in the fray.
If not, their might is greater than mine:
they'll break me in fragments and put me to flight,
intending to plunder what I must protect.
I can foil them if my fins are not frail,
and the rocks hold firm against my force.
You know my nature, now guess my name.

ANONYMOUS
Translated from the Anglo-Saxon by Kevin Crossley-Holland

Answer: anchor

SEA-
CHANGES

WHAT ARE HEAVY? SEA-SAND
AND SORROW

What are heavy? sea-sand and sorrow:
What are brief? to-day and to-morrow:
What are frail? Spring blossoms and youth:
What are deep? the ocean and truth.

CHRISTINA ROSSETTI

BLOW THE WIND WHISTLING

Up jumps the salmon
The largest o' em all
He jumps on our fore deck
Saying: Here's meat for all.
   O blow the wind whistling
   O blow the winds all
   Our ship is still hearted boys
   How steady she go!

Up jumps the shark
The largest of all
He jumped on our fore deck:
You should die all.

Then up jumps the sprat
The smallest of all
He jumps on our fore deck
Saying we shall be drowned all.

ANONYMOUS

still: perhaps a mis-hearing of the word 'steel'

SEA-CHANGE

'Goneys an' gullies an' all o' the birds o' the sea
   They ain't no birds, not really,' said Billy the Dane.
'Not mollies, nor gullies, nor goneys at all,' said he,
   'But simply the sperrits of mariners livin' again.

'Them birds goin' fishin' is nothin' but souls o' the
     drowned,
   Souls o' the drowned an' the kicked as are never no
     more
An' that there haughty old albatross cruisin' around,
   Belike he's Admiral Nelson or Admiral Noah.

'An' merry 's the life they are living. They settle and
     dip,
   They fishes, they never stands watches, they waggle
     their wings;
When a ship comes by, they fly to look at the ship
   To see how the nowaday mariners manages things.

'When freezing aloft in a snorter, I tell you I wish –
   (Though maybe it ain't like a Christian) – I wish I
     could be
A haughty old copper-bound albatross dipping for fish
   And coming the proud over all o' the birds o' the
     sea.'

JOHN MASEFIELD

goneys: albatrosses
gullies: sea-gulls
mollies: mollyhawks or fulmar petrels

GREAT BLACK-BACKED GULLS

Said Cap'n Morgan to Cap'n Kidd:
'Remember the grand times, Cap'n, when
The Jolly Roger flapped on the tropic breeze,
And we were the terrors of the Spanish Main?'
And Cap'n Kidd replied: 'Aye when our restless souls
Were steeped in human flesh and bone;
But now we range the seven seas, and fight
For galley scraps that men throw overboard.'

Two black-backed gulls, that perched
On a half-sunken spar –
Their eyes were gleaming-cold and through
The morning fog that crept upon the grey-green waves
Their wicked laughter sounded.

JOHN HEATH-STUBBS

Cap'n Morgan (Sir Henry Morgan, *c.* 1635–88) and Cap'n Kidd (William Kidd, *c.* 1645–1701) were two of the most notorious buccaneers in the history of piracy. At the time of his death, however, Morgan had become Lieutenant-Governor of Jamaica. Kidd was hanged at Execution Dock, on London's River Thames. Just why the black pirate-flag decorated with a white skull and cross-bones became known as the 'Jolly Roger' is unknown. The Spanish Main (mainland) stretched along the American coast from the Isthmus of Panama to the mouth of the River Orinoco, and the description also included that particular area of the Caribbean Sea alongside it.

THE MOONWUZO'S SEA-SONG

Who is that walking on the dark sea sand?
The old Bride of the Wind

What is that staring out of the weedy pool?
The newborn Monster in its caul

What is that eerie chanting from the foam?
The mermaid's gardening song

What is that shadow floating on the water?
The Fish-King's daughter

Who bears those candles down by the Sea's curled rim?
The children going home

CARA LOCKHART SMITH

caul: part of the membrane enclosing a child's head when it is born, and once believed to be a lucky charm against drowning

LOWLANDS

I dreamt a dream the other night,
  Lowlands, hurrah, my John;
I dreamt I saw my own true love,
  My Lowlands a-ray.

He was green and wet with weeds so-cold,
  Lowlands, hurrah, my John;
'I am drowned in the Lowland seas,' he said,
  My Lowlands a-ray.

'I shall never kiss you again,' he said,
  Lowlands, hurrah, my John;
I will cut away my bonny hair,
  My Lowlands a-ray.

No other man shall think me fair,
  Lowlands, hurrah, my John;
O my love lies drowned in the windy Lowlands,
  My Lowlands a-ray.

ANONYMOUS

This is a halliards chanty, sung while raising or lowering sail, yard, etc.

THE SAILOR'S MOTHER

  'O whence do you come,
Figure in the night-fog that chills me numb?'

'I come to you across from my house up there,
And I don't mind the brine-mist clinging to me
  That blows from the quay,
For I heard him in my chamber, and thought you
    unaware.'

  'But what did you hear,
That brought you blindly knocking in this middle-
    watch so drear?'

'My sailor son's voice as 'twere calling at your door,
And I don't mind my bare feet clammy on the stones,
  And the blight to my bones,
For he only knows of *this* house I lived in before.'

175

'Nobody's nigh,
Woman like a skeleton, with socket-sunk eye.'

'Ah – nobody's nigh! And my life is drearisome,
And this is the old home we loved in many a day
    Before he went away;
And the salt fog mops me. And nobody's come!'

THOMAS HARDY

TO THE MERMAID AT ZENNOR

Half fish, half fallen angel, none of you
Human at all – cease your lust's
Cold and insatiate crying from the tangled bay;
Nor, sea-hag, here
Stretch webbed and skinny fingers for your prey.

This is a hideous and a wicked country,
Sloping to hateful sunsets and the end of time,
Hollow with mine-shafts, naked with granite, fanatic
With sorrow. Abortions of the past
Hop through these bogs; black-faced, the villagers
Remember burnings by the hewn stones.

Only the saints,
Drifting on oak-leaves over the Irish Sea,
To sing like pipits from their crannied cells
With a thin stream of praise; who hear the Jennifer
Sob for her sins in a purgatory of foam –
Only these holy men

Can send you slithering from the chancel steps,
And wriggling back to your sunken paradise
Among the hollow-eyed and the capsized.

JOHN HEATH-STUBBS

Zennor is a coastal parish, once renowned for its fine singers, in the far west of Cornwall. Here, it is said, a mermaid lived for many generations, and one day fell in love with a choir-man who sang so beautifully that she took to attending church regularly, dressed as a fine lady. Finally, the tale goes on, she persuaded him to follow her into the sea, after which neither was seen nor heard of again. In the village church, dedicated to the virgin Saint Sinara or Senar, a 15th-century bench-end has a carving of a mermaid with a comb and a mirror.

In about the 5th century, many Irish missionaries, converts of St Patrick, came to Cornwall by various means. St Ia (St Ives), for example, is said to have arrived in a coracle, or even floating on a leaf.

Jennifer is the Cornish version of the name Guinevere, the legendary King Arthur's unfaithful Queen, who later bitterly repented and, heart-broken, spent her last years in a nunnery.

CHILDREN DEAR, WAS IT YESTERDAY

Children dear, was it yesterday
(Call yet once) that she went away?
Once she sat with you and me,
On a red-gold throne in the heart of the sea,
And the youngest sat on her knee.
She combed its bright hair, and she tended it well,
When down swung the sound of the far-off bell.
She sighed, she looked up through the clear green sea,
She said, 'I must go, for my kinsfolk pray
In the little gray church on the shore today.
'Twill be Easter time in the world – ah me!
And I lose my poor soul, Merman, here with thee.'
I said, 'Go up, dear heart, through the waves:

177

Say thy prayer, and come back to the kind sea caves.'
She smiled, she went up through the surf in the bay,
  Children dear, was it yesterday?

  Children dear, were we long alone?
'The sea grows stormy, the little ones moan;
Long prayers,' I said, 'in the world they say.'
'Come,' I said, and we rose through the surf in the bay.
We went up the beach, by the sandy down
Where the sea stocks bloom, to the white-walled town,
Through the narrow paved streets, where all was still,
To the little gray church on the windy hill.
From the church came a murmur of folk at their
       prayers,
But we stood without in the cold blowing airs.
We climbed on the graves, on the stones worn with
       rains,
And we gazed up the aisle through the small leaded
       panes.
  She sat by the pillar; we saw her clear:
  'Margaret, hist! come quick, we are here.
  Dear heart,' I said, 'we are alone.
  The sea grows stormy, the little ones moan.'
  But, ah, she gave me never a look,
  For her eyes were sealed to the holy book.
  Loud prays the priest; shut stands the door.
    Come away, children, call no more,
    Come away, come down, call no more.

Down, down, down,
Down to the depths of the sea.
She sits at her wheel in the humming town,
  Singing most joyfully.

Hark what she sings: 'O joy, O joy,
For the humming street, and the child with its toy!
For the priest, and the bell, and the holy well,
　　For the wheel where I spun,
　　And the blessed light of the sun!'
　　And so she sings her fill,
　　Singing most joyfully,
　　Till the shuttle falls from her hand,
　　And the whizzing wheel stands still.
She steals to the window, and looks at the sand,
　　And over the sand at the sea;
　　And her eyes are set in a stare;
　　And anon there breaks a sign,
　　And anon there drops a tear,
　　From a sorrow-clouded eye,
　　And a heart sorrow-laden,
　　　A long, long sigh,
　　For the cold strange eyes of a little Mermaiden
　　And the gleam of her golden hair.

MATTHEW ARNOLD
From *The Forsaken Merman*

Margaret, a mortal ('but faithless was she'), has returned to the world
leaving the Merman and their children beneath 'the clear green sea'.

THE SEA IS LOTH TO LOSE A FRIEND

　　The Sea is loth to lose a friend;
　　Men of one voyage, who did spend
　　Six months with him, hear his vexed cry
　　Haunting their houses till they die.

And for the sake of him they let
The winds blow them, and raindrops wet
Their foreheads with fresh water sprays –
Thinking of his wild, salty days.
And well they love to saunter near
A river, and its motion hear;
And see ships lying in calm beds,
That danced upon seas' living heads;
And in their dreams they hear again
Men's voices in a hurricane –
Like ghosts complaining that their graves
Are moved by sacrilegious waves.
And they do love to stand and hear
The old seafaring men that fear
Land more than water; carts and trains
More than wild waves and hurricanes.
And they do walk with love and pride
The tattooed mariner beside –
Chains, anchors on his arm, and Ships –
And listen to his bearded lips.
Aye, they will hear the Sea's vexed cry
Haunting their houses till they die.

W. H. DAVIES
From *The Call of the Sea*

A KISS OF A SEA-MAN IS
WORTH TWO OF ANOTHER

When first I chanc't to be among them,
I was belov'd of divers young men;
And with a modest mild behaviour
They did intreat my love and favour.
  But this I learned from my mother,
  A kiss of a Sea-man's worth two of another.

Brave gentlemen of rank and fashion,
That live, most richly in the Nation,
Have woo'd and su'd, as brave as may be,
That I might have been a pretty Lady.
  Love's fiery beams I cannot smother,
  A kiss of a Sea-man's worth two of another.

ANONYMOUS

Blare: perhaps either 'loud-mouthed,' like a trumpet, or 'dazzlingly
  brilliant' as with the 'blare' of a bright colour; but the precise meaning
  is uncertain.

THE SAUCY SAILOR BOY

Come, my only one, come, my fond one,
Come, my dearest, unto me.
Won't you wed with this poor sailor boy
Just returnèd from the sea?

No, you're a ragged love, no, a dirty love
And you smells so strong of tar.
You be gone, you saucy sailor boy,
You be gone, you Jack-tar.

If I am a ragged love, if I'm a dirty love,
If I smell so strong of tar,
I have silver in my pocket, love,
And I've gold all in bright store.

So soon as she heard him say it,
On her bended knees she fell
Saying, I'll wed with my dear Henery
For I love my jolly sailor well.

No, I'd rather cross the briny oceans
Where there's no field to be seen.
Since you've refused the offer, love,
Some other shall wear the ring.

ANONYMOUS

SHIP AHOY!

When the Man-o'-War or Merchant ship
Comes sailing into Port,
The Jolly Tar with joy,
Will sing out 'Land a-hoy!'
With his pockets full of money
And a parrot in a cage,
He smiles at all the pretty girls
Upon the landing stage.

Chorus All the nice girls love a sailor,
All the nice girls love a tar;
For there's something about a sailor,
Well, you know what sailors are.
Bright and breezy, free and easy,
He's the ladies' pride and joy;
Falls in love with Kate and Jane,
Then he's off to sea again,
Ship a-hoy! ship a-hoy!

Jack is partial to the yellow girls
Across the Eastern Seas;
With lovely almond eyes
The tar they hypnotise
And when he goes to the Sandwich Isles
He loves the dusky belles,
Dress'd up *à la* Salome,
Coloured beads and oyster shells.

Chorus All the nice girls love a sailor, etc.

A. J. MILLS

The music for this music-hall song was composed by Bennett Scott.

THE SAILOR AND THE SHARK

There was a queen that fell in love with a jolly sailor
bold,
But he shipped to the Indies, where he would seek for
gold.
*All in a good sea-boat, my boys, we fear no wind that
blows!*

There was a king that had a fleet of ships both tall and
tarred;
He carried off this pretty queen, and she jumped
overboard.
*All in a good sea-boat, my boys, we fear no wind that
blows!*

The queen, the queen is overboard! a shark was
cruising round,
He swallowed up this dainty bit alive and safe and
sound.
*All in a good sea-boat, my boys, we fear no wind that
blows!*

Within the belly of this shark it was both dark and
cold,
But she was faithful still and true to her jolly sailor
bold.
*All in a good sea-boat, my boys, we fear no wind that
blows!*

The shark was sorry for her, and swam away so fast.
In the Indies, where the camels are, he threw her up at
last.
*All in a good sea-boat, my boys, we fear no wind that
blows!*

On one of these same goodly beasts, all in a palanquin,
She spied her own true love again – The Emperor of
   Tonquin.
All in a good sea-boat, my boys, we fear no wind that
   blows!

She called to him, 'O stay, my love, your queen is
   come, my dear.'
'Oh I've a thousand queens more fair within my
   kingdom here.'
All in a good sea-boat, my boys, we fear no wind that
   blows!

'You smell of the grave so strong, my dear.' 'I've sailed
   in a shark,' says she.
'It is not of the grave I smell; but I smell of the fish of
   the sea.'
All in a good sea-boat, my boys, we fear no wind that
   blows!

'My lady loves they smell so sweet; of rice-powder so
   fine.
The queen the King of Paris loves no sweeter smells
   than mine.'
All in a good sea-boat, my boys, we fear no wind that
   blows!

She got aboard the shark again, and weeping went her
   way;
The shark swam back again so fast to where the tall
   ships lay.
All in a good sea-boat, my boys, we fear no wind that
   blows!

The king he got the queen again, the shark away he
  swam.
The queen was merry as could be, and mild as any lamb.
All in a good sea-boat, my boys, we fear no wind that
  blows!

* * * *

Now all you pretty maidens what love a sailor bold,
You'd better ship along with him before his love grows
  cold.

FREDERICK YORK POWELL
From the French of Paul Fort

A BALLAD OF SIR FRANCIS DRAKE

Before Sir Francis put to sea,
He told his love, 'My dear,
When I am gone, you wait for me,
Though you wait for seven year.'

His love, who was redder than the rose,
And sweeter than the may,
Said, 'I will wait till summer snows
And winter fields bear hay.

'I'll wait until the ice is hot,
And July sun is cold,
Until the cliffs of Dover rot,
And the cliffs of Devon mould.'

Sir Francis went aboard his ship,
Her sails were sheeted home,
The water gurgled at her lip
And whitened into foam.

And months went by, but no more word
Came from that roving soul
Than comes from the Mother Carey bird
That nests at the South Pole.

In the seventh year men gave up hope,
And swore that he was dead.
They had the bell tolled with the rope
And the burial service read.

His love, who was redder than the rose,
Mourned for him long and long,
But even grief for a lover goes
When life is running strong.

And many a man beset her way
Who thought it Paradise
To gaze at her lovely eyes and say
That her eyes were stars, not eyes.

And so she promised a nobleman
When the ninth-year hay was hauled,
And before the harvest-home began
Her marriage banns were called.

The wedding-day came bright and fair,
The bells rang up and down,
The bridesmaids in their white were there
And the parson in his gown.

The rosy bride came up the aisle,
The page-boys bore her train;
She stood by the groom a little while
To be made one out of twain.

Not one of all within the church
Thought of Sir Francis Drake.
A crash made the transept columns lurch
And the central tower quake.

A cannon-ball came thundering by
Between the bride and groom.
The girl said 'Francis wonders why
There's someone in his room.

'Francis is homing from the seas,
He has sent this message here.
I would rather be wife to Francis, please,
Than the lady of a peer.'

Ere the priest could start his talk again,
A man rushed in to say,
'Here is Drake come home with the wealth
    of Spain.
His ships are in the Bay.'

The noble said with courtly grace,
'It would be a wiser plan
If I let Sir Francis take my place,
And I will be Best Man.'

JOHN MASEFIELD

Mother Carey bird: stormy petrel

THE PARROT

Long since I'd ceased to care
Though he should curse and swear
The little while he spent at home with me:
And yet I couldn't bear
To hear his parrot swear
The day I learned my man was drowned at sea.

He'd taught the silly bird
To jabber word for word
Outlandish oaths that he'd picked up at sea;
And now it seemed I heard
In every wicked word
The dead man from the deep still cursing me.

A flood of easing tears,
Though I'd not wept for years,
Brought back old long-forgotten dreams to me,
The foolish hopes and fears
Of the first half-happy years
Before his soul was stolen by the sea.

WILFRID GIBSON

THE MASTER, THE SWABBER,
THE BOATSWAIN, AND I

The master, the swabber, the boatswain, and I,
    The gunner, and his mate,
Lov'd Mall, Meg, and Marian, and Margery,
    But none of us car'd for Kate:
    For she had a tongue with a tang,
    Would cry to a sailor, Go hang!
    She lov'd not the savour of tar nor of pitch;
    Yet a tailor might scratch her where'er she did itch.
      Then to sea, boys, and let her go hang!

WILLIAM SHAKESPEARE
From *The Tempest*

THE SAILOR'S WIFE

And are ye sure the news is true?
    And are ye sure he's weel?
Is this a time to think o' wark?
    Ye jades, lay by your wheel;
Is this the time to spin a thread,
    When Colin's at the door?
Reach down my cloak, I'll to the quay,
    And see him come ashore.
For there's nae luck about the house,
    There's nae luck at a';
There's little pleasure in the house
    When our gudeman's awa'.

And gie to me my bigonet,
  My bishop's satin gown;
For I maun tell the baillie's wife
  That Colin's in the town.
My Turkey slippers maun gae on,
  My stockins pearly blue;
It's a' to pleasure our gudeman,
  For he's baith leal and true.

Rise, lass, and mak a clean fireside,
  Put on the muckle pot;
Gie little Kate her button gown
  And Jock his Sunday coat;
And mak their shoon as black as slaes,
  Their hose as white as snaw;
It's a' to please my ain gudeman,
  For he's been long awa'.

There's twa fat hens upo' the coop
  Been fed this month and mair;
Mak haste and thraw their necks about,
  That Colin weel may fare;
And spread the table neat and clean,
  Gar ilka thing look braw,
For wha can tell how Colin fared
  When he was far awa'?

Sae true his heart, sae smooth his speech,
  His breath like caller air;
His very foot has music in't
  As he comes up the stair –
And will I see his face again?
  And will I hear him speak?
I'm downright dizzy wi' the thought,
  In troth I'm like to greet!

If Colin's weel, and weel content,
    I hae nae mair to crave:
And gin I live to keep him sae,
    I'm blest aboon the lave:
And will I see his face again,
    And will I hear him speak?
I'm downright dizzy wi' the thought,
    In troth I'm like to greet.
For there's nae luck about the house,
    There's nae luck at a';
There's little pleasure in the house
    When our gudeman's awa'.

WILLIAM JULIUS MICKLE

jades: housewives; hussies (used in fun)
gudeman: husband
bigonet: a linen cap or coif, from the name of a hood worn by a Beguine
    lay-sister or nun
bishop's satin gown: a smart gown, one made of stylish material
maun: must
baillie: equivalent in Scotland of an Alderman
leal: loyal; true
muckle: big; large
slaes: sloes
thraw their necks about: wring their necks
gar ilka thing: make everything
caller: fresh and cool
aboon the lave: above all others

This song, also known as 'The Mariner's Wife' and 'There's Nae Luck about the House', was found among W. J. Mickle's papers and is claimed by his admirers as his work. Others believe it may have been written by Mrs Jean Adams (1710–65), a poet and schoolmistress of Crawford-dyke, near Greenock, Scotland. Robert Burns says it was sung on the streets as an anonymous ballad in about 1771 or 1772.

AT ST SIMEON'S SHRINE
I SAT DOWN TO WAIT

At St Simeon's shrine I sat down to wait,
The waves came nearer, the waves grew great,
   As I was awaiting my lover,
   As I was awaiting my lover!
There at St Simeon's shrine by the altar,
Greater and nearer, the waves did not falter,
   As I was awaiting my lover,
   As I was awaiting my lover!
As the waves drew nearer and greater grew,
There was no steersman nor rower in view,
   As I was awaiting my lover,
   As I was awaiting my lover!
The waves of the high sea nearer flow
There is no steersman, I cannot row
   As I am awaiting my lover,
   As I am awaiting my lover!
There is no steersman nor rower, and I
In the high sea in my beauty must die,
   As I am awaiting my lover,
   As I am awaiting my lover!
There is no steersman, no rower am I
And in the high sea my beauty must die,
   As I am awaiting my lover,
   As I am awaiting my lover.

MINDINHO
Translated from the Portuguese by Roy Campbell

MEETING AT NIGHT

The grey sea and the long black land;
And the yellow half-moon large and low;
And the startled little waves that leap
In fiery ringlets from their sleep,
As I gain the cove with pushing prow,
And quench its speed i' the slushy sand.

Then a mile of warm sea-scented beach;
Three fields to cross till a farm appears;
A tap at the pane, the quick sharp scratch
And blue spurt of a lighted match,
And a voice less loud, thro' its joys and fears,
Than the two hearts beating each to each!

ROBERT BROWNING

DREAMERS,
SOLITARIES &
SURVIVORS

MRS ARBUTHNOT

Mrs Arbuthnot was a poet
A poet of high degree,
But her talent left her;
Now she lives at home by the sea.

In the morning she washes up,
In the afternoon she sleeps,
Only in the evenings sometimes
For her lost talent she weeps,

Crying: I should write a poem,
Can I look a wave in the face
If I do not write a poem about a sea-wave,
Putting the words in place.

Mrs Arbuthnot has died,
She has gone to heaven,
She is one with the heavenly combers now
And need not write about them.

Cry: She is a heavenly comber,
She runs with a comb of fire,
Nobody writes or wishes to
Who is one with their desire.

STEVIE SMITH

ANGEL HILL

A sailor came walking down Angel Hill,
He knocked on my door with a right good will,
With a right good will he knocked on my door.
He said, 'My friend, we have met before.'
    No, never, said I.

He searched my eye with a sea-blue stare
And he laughed aloud on the Cornish air,
On the Cornish air he laughed aloud
And he said, 'My friend, you have grown too proud.'
    No, never, said I.

'In war we swallowed the bitter bread
And drank of the brine,' the sailor said.
'We took of the bread and we tasted the brine
As I bound your wounds and you bound mine.'
    No, never, said I.

'By day and night on the diving sea
We whistled to sun and moon,' said he.
'Together we whistled to moon and sun
And vowed our stars should be as one.'
    No, never, said I.

'And now,' he said, 'that the war is past
I come to your hearth and home at last.
I come to your home and hearth to share
Whatever fortune waits me there.'
    No, never, said I.

'I have no wife nor son,' he said,
'Nor pillow on which to lay my head,
No pillow have I, nor wife nor son,
Till you shall give to me my own.'
    No, never, said I.

His eye it flashed like a lightning-dart
And still as a stone then stood my heart.
My heart as a granite stone was still
And he said, 'My friend, but I think you will.'
    No, never, said I.

The sailor smiled and turned in his track
And shifted the bundle on his back
And I heard him sing as he strolled away,
'You'll send and you'll fetch me one fine day.'
    No, never, said I.

CHARLES CAUSLEY

THE SOLITUDE OF
ALEXANDER SELKIRK

I am monarch of all I survey;
My right there is none to dispute;
From the centre all round to the sea
I am lord of the fowl and the brute.
O Solitude! where are the charms
That sages have seen in thy face?
Better dwell in the midst of alarms
Than reign in this horrible place.

I am out of humanity's reach,
I must finish my journey alone,
Never hear the sweet music of speech;
I start at the sound of my own.
The beasts that roam over the plain
My form with indifference see;
They are so unacquainted with man,
Their tameness is shocking to me.

Society, Friendship and Love
Divinely bestow'd upon man,
O had I the wings of a dove
How soon would I taste you again!
My sorrows I then might assuage
In the ways of religion and truth,
Might learn from the wisdom of age,
And be cheer'd by the sallies of youth.

Religion! What treasure untold
Resides in that heavenly word!
More precious than silver and gold,
Or all that this earth can afford.
But the sound of the church-going bell
These valleys and rocks never heard,
Never sigh'd at the sound of a knell,
Or smiled when a sabbath appear'd.

Ye winds that have made me your sport,
Convey to this desolate shore
Some cordial endearing report
Of a land I shall visit no more:

My friends, do they now and then send
A wish or a thought after me?
O tell me I yet have a friend,
Though a friend I am never to see.

How fleet is a glance of the mind!
Compared with the speed of its flight,
The tempest itself lags behind,
And the swift-wingéd arrows of light.
When I think of my own native land
In a moment I seem to be there;
But alas! recollection at hand
Soon hurries me back to despair.

But the seafowl is gone to her nest,
The beast is laid down in his lair;
Even here is a season of rest,
And I to my cabin repair.
There's mercy in every place,
And mercy, encouraging thought!
Gives even affliction a grace
And reconciles man to his lot.

WILLIAM COWPER

Alexander Selkirk (1676–1721), son of a shoemaker of Fife in Scotland, ran off to sea and joined a privateering expedition. After quarrelling with his captain, he asked to be put ashore on the uninhabited island of Juan Fernandez in the South Pacific in 1704. He stayed there for four years and four months until rescued by Captain Woodes Rogers, who told the story in his book *A Cruising Voyage Round the World* (1712). From this, Daniel Defoe is said to have been inspired to write *The Life and strange surprising Adventures of Robinson Crusoe* (1719). Defoe, who is thought never to have met Selkirk, seems to have placed his story in Tobago, but never visited the West Indies.

SYNGE ON ARAN

Salt off the sea whets
the blades of four winds.
They peel acres
of locked rock, pare down
a rind of shrivelled ground;
bull-noses are chiselled
on cliffs.
          Islanders too
are for sculpting. Note
the pointed scowl, the mouth
carved as upturned anchor
and the polished head
full of drownings.
             There
he comes now, a hard pen
scraping in his head;
the nib filed on a salt wind
and dipped in the keening sea.

SEAMUS HEANEY

keening: wailing; the sound that accompanies the singing of a keen, or
   Irish funeral song

The Irish playwright John Millington Synge (1871–1909) often visited
the Aran Isles, in Galway Bay. Two of his most well-known plays are
Riders to the Sea and *The Playboy of the Western World*. In a comic poem
Synge wrote called 'The Curse', about someone who disapproved of *The
Playboy*, he also shows us how to pronounce his surname:

'Lord, this judgment quickly bring,
And I'm your servant, J. M. Synge.'

SHIPWRECK, STORM AND DISASTER

THE VALUE OF GOLD TO SAILORS

'We've ransacked the town,' the pirates said,
'We've left half the people injured, the other half dead.
We've plundered their gold and stolen their jewels,
It was easy attacking such trusting fools.
The only thing they put up a real fight for
Was some useless wood down on the shore.'

But when the gold-laden boat danced into a storm,
When the shroud-like sails became useless and torn,
When their faces turned ashen, bewildered and pale,
In their hearts then the jewels grew stale.
And as each pirate panicked, drowning he swore
He had meant to bring the wood seen on the sea-shore.

BRIAN PATTEN
Adapted from Aesop's Fable *The Piece of Wood*

WRECK OF THE RAFT

Even as he spoke, a monstrous wave abaft
Came towering up, and crashed into the raft:
And the raft heeled, and off it far he fell,
And from his hand shot out the rudder-shaft.

And in one whirling gust the hurricane
Snapped the mast midway; far into the main
Fell top and rigging: and beneath the surge
He sank, nor for a while his head again

Out of the overwhelming wave could lift:
For now the raiment, bright Calypso's gift,
Weighed heavy on him: but at last he rose,
And with abundant-streaming head made shift

Out of his mouth to spit the salt sea-spray.
Yet withal marking where the wrecked raft lay,
He plunged amid the waves and caught at it,
And crouched amidships, keeping death at bay:

While the raft helpless on the tideway spun,
As down the plain when Autumn is begun,
Before the North wind tufts of thistledown
Entangled close together twirling run;

So him across the sea in furious race
Hither and thither the winds bore apace:
And now south wind to north its plaything tossed,
And now east wind to west gave up the chase.

HOMER
From *The Odyssey*, Book V
Translated from the Greek by J. W. Mackail

The Odyssey tells of the adventures of Odysseus (Ulysses) as he voyaged
home to Ithaca after the Trojan War.

BUT INO OF THE SLIM ANKLES
HAD SEEN HIM

But Ino of the slim ankles had seen him, – Ino the bright, a daughter of Cadmus. She had been born mortal in the beginning: just a simple-speaking girl: but she had attained honour amongst the gods and now was made free of wide ocean's salty depths. She pitied Odysseus so carried to and fro in anguish. Easily, like a sea gull, she rose from the level of the sea to light on the raft and say, 'Unhappy man, why is Poseidon so cruelly provoked against you as to plant these many harms in your path? Yet shall you not wholly perish, for all his eager hate. See: – if, as I think, you are understanding, this is what you must do. Strip off these clothes that are upon you and abandon the raft to go with the winds, while instead you try by swimming to gain the Phaeacian shore, your destined safety. Further, take this divine veil of mine and strain it round your chest. While you wear it you need not be harmed, or die: and afterwards, when you have solid land in your possession, unbind the veil from you and fling it far out from shore into the wine-dark sea, yourself turning away the while.'

The goddess spoke, gave him the scarf, and with bird-swiftness sprang back again into the breakers: and the blackness of the water closed over her.

HOMER
From *The Odyssey*, Book V
Translated from the Greek by T. E. Shaw (T. E. Lawrence)

In 1927 T. E. Lawrence, or 'Lawrence of Arabia', changed his name by Deed Poll to T. E. Shaw. While serving as an aircraftman in the Royal Air Force, he made a translation of *The Odyssey of Homer*, and it was published in 1935.

SWIFTER AND SWIFTER THE
WHITE SHIP SPED

Swifter and swifter the *White Ship* sped
Till she flew as the spirit flies from the dead:

As white as a lily glimmered she
Like a ship's fair ghost upon the sea.

And the Prince cried, 'Friends, 'tis the hour to sing!
Is a songbird's course so swift on the wing?'

And under the winter's stars' still throng,
From brown throats, white throats, merry and strong,
The knights and the ladies raised a song.

A song – nay, a shriek that rent the sky,
That leaped o'er the deep! – the grievous cry
Of three hundred living that now must die:

An instant shriek that sprang to the shock
As the ship's keel felt the sunken rock.

A moment the pilot's senses spin –
The next he snatched the Prince 'mid the din,
Cut the boat loose, and the youth leaped in.

A few friends leaped with him, standing near.
'Row! the sea's smooth and the night is clear!'

'What! none to be saved but these and I?'
'Row, row as you'd live! All here must die!'

Out of the churn of the choking ship,
Which the gulf grapples and the waves strip,
They struck with the strained oars' flash and dip.

'Twas then o'er the splitting bulwarks' brim
The Prince's sister screamed to him.

He gazed aloft, still rowing apace,
And through the whirled surf he knew her face.

To the toppling decks clave one and all
As a fly cleaves to a chamber-wall.

I Berold was clinging anear;
I prayed for myself and quaked with fear,
But I saw his eyes as he looked at her.

He knew her face and he heard her cry
And he said, 'Put back! she must not die!'

And back with the current's force they reel
Like a leaf that's drawn to a water-wheel.

'Neath the ship's travail they scarce might float,
But he rose and stood in the rocking boat.

Low the poor ship leaned on the tide:
O'er the naked keel as she best might slide,
The sister toiled to the brother's side.

He reached an oar to her from below,
And stiffened his arms to clutch her so.

But now from the ship some spied the boat,
And 'Saved!' was the cry from many a throat.

And down to the boat they leaped and fell:
It turned as a bucket turns in a well,
And nothing was there but the surge and swell.

The Prince that was and the King to come,
There in an instant gone to his doom.

He was a Prince of lust and pride;
He showed no grace till the hour he died.

When he should be King, he oft would vow,
He'd yoke the peasant to his own plough.
O'er him the ships score their furrows now.

God only knows where his soul did wake,
But I saw him die for his sister's sake.

By none but me can the tale be told,
The butcher of Rouen, poor Berold.
    (*Lands are swayed by a King on a throne.*)
'Twas a royal train put forth to sea,
Yet the tale can be told by none but me.
    (*The sea hath no King but God alone.*)

DANTE GABRIEL ROSSETTI
From *The White Ship*

Prince William, the son of King Henry I and grandson of William the Conqueror, was drowned in 1120 in the loss of the *White Ship* when taking passage from Normandy to England, and while trying to rescue his half-sister. The story in Rossetti's poem is told by a sole survivor.

THE COINER
(CIRCA 1611)

Against the Bermudas we foundered, whereby
This Master, that Swabber, yon Bo'sun, and I
(Our pinnace and crew being drowned in the main)
Must beg for our bread through old England again.

For a bite and a sup, and a bed of clean straw,
We'll tell you such marvels as man never saw,
On a Magical Island which no one did spy
Save this Master, that Swabber, yon Bo'sun, and I.

Seven months among Mermaids and Devils and Sprites,
And Voices that howl in the cedars o' nights,
With further enchantments we underwent there.
Good Sirs, 'tis a tale to draw guts from a bear!

'Twixt Dover and Southwark it paid us our way,
Where we found some poor players were labouring a
    play;
And, willing to search what such business might be,
We entered the yard, both to hear and to see.

One hailed us for seamen and courteous-ly
Did guide us apart to a tavern near by
Where we told him our tale (as to many of late),
And he gave us good cheer, so we gave him good
    weight.

Mulled sack and strong waters on bellies well lined
With beef and black pudding do strengthen the mind;
And seeing him greedy for marvels, at last
From plain salted truth to flat leasing we passed.

But he, when on midnight our reckoning he paid,
Says, 'Never match coins with a Coiner by trade,
Or he'll turn your lead pieces to metal as rare
As shall fill him this globe, and leave something to
  spare. . .'

We slept where they laid us, and when we awoke
'Was a crown or five shillings in every man's poke.
We bit them and rang them, and, finding them good,
We drank to that Coiner as honest men should!

For a cup and a crust, and a truss, etc.

RUDYARD KIPLING

A coiner is one who makes coins, but here it refers to William Shakespeare.
His last play, *The Tempest*, is believed to be partly based on a famous ship-
wreck in the Bermudas in 1609, and was probably written in about 1609.

ALL LOST! TO PRAYERS,
TO PRAYERS! ALL LOST!

(SCENE: ON A SHIP AT SEA)
Enter Mariners, wet

MARINERS All lost! to prayers, to prayers! all lost!

BOATSWAIN What, must our mouths be cold?

GONZALO The king and prince at prayers! let us assist
    them,
For our case is as theirs.

SEBASTIAN I am out of patience.

ANTONIO We are merely cheated of our lives by
    drunkards. –
This wide-chapp'd rascal, – would thou might'st lie
    drowning,
The washing of ten tides!

GONZALO He'll be hang'd yet,
Though every drop of water swear against it,
And gape at wid'st to glut him.
A confused noise, within: – 'Mercy on us!' –
'We split, we split!' – 'Farewell, my wife and
    children!' –
'Farewell, brother!' – 'We split, we split, we split!' –

ANTONIO Let's all sink wi' the king.   *Exit*

SEBASTIAN Let's take leave of him.   *Exit*

GONZALO Now would I give a thousand furlongs of sea
for an acre of barren ground; long heath, broom, furze,
anything. The wills above be done! but I would fain
die a dry death.   *Exeunt*

WILLIAM SHAKESPEARE
From *The Tempest*

washing of ten tides: the punishment for piracy was to be hanged at low
  water mark and left while three tides flowed and ebbed

AND NOW THE STORM-BLAST CAME

'And now the Storm-blast came,
    and he
Was tyrannous and strong:
He struck with his o'ertaking wings,
And chased us south along.

The ship driven by a storm toward the South Pole.

'With sloping masts and dipping prow,
As who pursued with yell and blow
Still treads the shadow of his foe,
And forward bends his head,
The ship drove fast, loud roar'd the
    blast,
And southward aye we fled.

'And now there came both mist and
    snow,
And it grew wondrous cold:
And ice, mast-high, came floating by,
As green as emerald.

'And through the drifts the snowy
    clifts
Did send a dismal sheen:
Nor shapes of men nor beasts we
    ken –
The ice was all between.

The land of ice, and of fearful sounds, where no living thing was to be seen.

'The ice was here, the ice was there,
The ice was all around:
It crack'd and growl'd, and roar'd
    and howl'd,
Like noises in a swound!

'At length did cross an Albatross,
Thorough the fog it came;
As if it had been a Christian soul,
We hail'd it in God's name.

Till a great sea-bird,
called the Albatross,
came through the snow-
fog, and was received
with great joy and hos-
pitality.

'It ate the food it ne'er had eat,
And round and round it flew.
The ice did split with a thunder-fit;
The helmsman steer'd us through!

'And a good south wind sprung up
    behind;
The Albatross did follow,
And every day, for food or play,
Came to the mariners' hollo!

And lo! the Albatross
proveth a bird of good
omen, and followeth the
ship as it returned north-
ward through fog and
floating ice.

'In mist or cloud, on mast or shroud,
It perch'd for vespers nine;
Whiles all the night, through fog-
    smoke white,
Glimmer'd the white moonshine.'

'God save thee, ancient Mariner,
From the fiends, that plague thee
    thus! –
Why look'st thou so?' – 'With my
    crossbow
I shot the Albatross.

The ancient Mariner
inhospitably killeth the
pious bird of good omen.

'The Sun now rose upon the right:
Out of the sea came he,
Still hid in mist, and on the left
Went down into the sea.

'And the good south wind still blew
  behind,
But no sweet bird did follow,
Nor any day for food or play
Came to the mariners' hollo!

'And I had done a hellish thing,
And it would work 'em woe:
For all averr'd I had kill'd the bird
That made the breeze to blow.
Ah wretch! said they, the bird to
  slay,
That made the breeze to blow!

His shipmates cry out against the ancient Mariner for killing the bird of good luck.

'Nor dim nor red, like God's own
  head,
The glorious Sun uprist:
Then all averr'd I had kill'd the bird
That brought the fog and mist.
'Twas right, said they, such birds to
  slay,
That bring the fog and mist.

But when the fog cleared off, they justify the same, and thus make themselves accomplices in the crime.

'The fair breeze blew, the white
  foam flew,
The furrow follow'd free;
We were the first that ever burst
Into that silent sea.

The fair breeze continues; the ship enters the Pacific Ocean, and sails northward, even till it reaches the Line.

'Down dropt the breeze, the sails
  dropt down,
'Twas sad as sad could be;
And we did speak only to break
The silence of the sea!

The ship hath been suddenly becalmed.

'All in a hot and copper sky,
The bloody Sun, at noon,
Right up above the mast did stand,
No bigger than the Moon.

'Day after day, day after day,
We stuck, nor breath nor motion;
As idle as a painted ship
Upon a painted ocean.

'Water, water, everywhere,　　　　　*And the Albatross*
And all the boards did shrink;　　　*begins to be avenged.*
Water, water, everywhere
Nor any drop to drink.'

SAMUEL TAYLOR COLERIDGE
From *The Rime of the Ancient Mariner*

vespers: here, evenings; period of evening prayers; Vesper is also Hes-
  perus, the evening star

In Coleridge's complete poem, first published in 1798 and originally based
on a dream told him by a friend and on the many versions which he had
studied of the legend that it is fatal to shoot an albatross, all the ship's
company finally die of thirst except the guilty mariner who tells the story.
In a moonlit vision, he then sees 'God's creatures of the great calm', and
as a penance for his crime is condemned to travel the world and teach
'by his own example, love and reverence to all things that God made and
loveth' so that all might more fully understand the mystical fellowship
and unity of 'man and bird and beast'.

> 'He prayeth best, who loveth best
>   All things both great and small;
>   For the dear God who loveth us,
>   He made and loveth all.'

PETER GRIMES' THIRD APPRENTICE

Passive he labour'd, till his slender frame
Bent with his loads, and he at length was lame:
Strange that a frame so weak could bear so long
The grossest insult and the foulest wrong;
But there were causes – in the town they gave
Fire, food, and comfort, to the gentle slave;
And though stern Peter, with a cruel hand,
And knotted rope, enforced the rude command,
Yet he consider'd what he'd lately felt,
And his vile blows with selfish pity dealt.
One day such draughts the cruel fisher made,
He could not vend them in his borough-trade,
But sail'd for London-mart: the boy was ill,
But ever humbled to his master's will;
And on the river, where they smoothly sail'd,
He strove with terror and awhile prevail'd;
But new to danger on the angry sea,
He clung affrighten'd to his master's knee:
The boat grew leaky and the wind was strong,
Rough was the passage and the time was long;
His liquor fail'd, and Peter's wrath arose, –
No more is known – the rest we must suppose,
Or learn of Peter; – Peter says, he 'spied
The stripling's danger and for harbour tried;
Meantime the fish, and then th' apprentice died.'
The pitying women raised a clamour round,
And weeping said, 'Thou hast thy 'prentice drown'd.'
Now the stern man was summon'd to the hall,
To tell his tale before the burghers all:
He gave th' account; profess'd the lad he loved,
And kept his brazen features all unmoved.

The mayor himself with tone severe replied, –
'Henceforth with thee shall never boy abide;
Hire thee a freeman, whom thou durst not beat,
But who, in thy despite, will sleep and eat:
Free thou art now! – again shouldst thou appear,
Thou'lt find thy sentence, like thy soul, severe.'

GEORGE CRABBE
From *The Borough*

The composer Benjamin Britten made George Crabbe's story of Peter Grimes the basis of one of his earliest and most celebrated operas, written in California between January 1944 and February 1945, with a libretto prepared by Montagu Slater. In a note* on how he came to write the opera, Benjamin Britten said, 'For most of my life I have lived closely in touch with the sea. My parents' house in Lowestoft directly faced the sea, and my life as a child was coloured by the fierce storms that sometimes drove ships on to our coast and ate away whole stretches of the neighbouring cliffs. In writing *Peter Grimes*, I wanted to express my awareness of the perpetual struggle of men and women whose livelihood depends on the sea. . .'

* *Peter Grimes*, essays on the opera edited by Eric Crozier (Bodley Head, 1945)

THE FIGURE-HEAD OF THE *CALEDONIA* AT HER CAPTAIN'S GRAVE

We laid them in their lowly rest,
  The strangers of a distant shore;
We smoothed the green turf on their breast,
  'Mid baffled Ocean's angry roar;
And there, the relique of the storm,
We fixed fair Scotland's figured form.

She watches by her bold, her brave,
  Her shield towards the fatal sea:
Their cherished lady of the wave
  Is guardian of their memory.
Stern is her look, but calm, for there
No gale can rend or billow bear.

Stand, silent image! stately stand,
  Where sighs shall breathe and tears be shed,
And many a heart of Cornish land,
  Will soften for the stranger dead.
They came in paths of storm; they found
This quiet home in Christian ground.

ROBERT STEPHEN HAWKER

The *Caledonia*, 200 tons, homeward bound with a cargo of wheat from Odessa on the Black Sea, was wrecked in a hurricane and broken to pieces on the rocks at Sharp's Nose, Morwenstow, North Cornwall, in 1842. Only one member of the crew of ten was saved. The ship's white figure-head still stands in the churchyard. 'Caledonia' was the Roman name for part of northern Britain, and today signifies Scotland.

THE WHALE

O, 'twas in the year of ninety four,
And of June the second day,
That our gallant ship her anchor weighed
And from Stromness bore away, brave boys!
    And from Stromness bore away!

Now Speedicut was our captain's name,
And our ship the *Lion* bold,
And we were bound to far Greenland,
To the land of ice and cold – brave boys,
    To the land of ice and cold.

And when we came to far Greenland,
And to Greenland cold came we,
Where there's ice, and there's snow, and the
        whalefishes blow,
We found all open sea – brave boys,
    We found all open sea.

Then the mate he climbed to the crow's nest high,
With his spy-glass in his hand,
'There's a whale, there's a whale, there's a whalefish,'
        he cried,
'And she blows at every span' – brave boys,
    She blows at every span.

Our captain stood on his quarter-deck,
And a fine little man was he.
'Overhaul, overhaul, on your davit tackle fall,
And launch your boats to the sea' – brave boys,
    And launch your boats to the sea.

Now the boats were launched and the men a-board,
With the whalefish full in view;
Resol-ved were the whole boats' crews
To steer where the whalefish blew – brave boys,
    To steer where the whalefish blew.

And when we reached that whale, my boys,
He lashed out with his tail,
And we lost a boat, and seven good men,
And we never caught that whale – brave boys,
    And we never caught that whale.

Bad new, bad news, to our captain came,
That grieved him very sore.
But when he found that his cabin-boy was gone,
Why it grieved him ten times more – brave boys,
    It grieved him ten times more.

O, Greenland is an awful place,
Where the daylight's seldom seen,
Where there's ice, and there's snow, and the
        whalefishes blow,
Then *adieu* to cold Greenland – brave boys,
    Adieu to cold Greenland.

ANONYMOUS

davit tackle: gear on a pair of uprights, curved at the top, for suspending
    or lowering a boat

PAT CLOHERTY'S VERSION OF
THE MAISIE

I've no tooth to sing you the song
    Tierney made at the time
      but I'll tell the truth

It happened on St John's Day
    sixty-eight years ago
      last June the twenty-fourth

The Maisie sailed from Westport Quay
    homeward on a Sunday
      missing Mass to catch the tide

John Kerrigan sat at her helm
    Michael Barrett stood at her mast
      and Kerrigan's wife lay down below

The men were two stepbrothers
    drownings in the family
      and all through the family

Barrett kept a shop in the island
    Kerrigan plied the hooker
      now deeply laden with flour

She passed Clare and she came to Cahir
    two reefs tied in the mainsail
      she bore a foresail but no jib

South-east wind with strong ebb-tide
    still she rode this way that way
      hugging it hugging it O my dear

And it blew and blew hard and blew hard
  but Kerrigan kept her to it
    as long as he was there he kept her to it

Rain fell in a cloudburst
  hailstones hit her deck
    there was no return for him once he'd put out

At Inishturk when the people saw
  The Maisie smothered up in darkness
    they lit candles in the church

What more could Kerrigan do?
  he put her jaw into the hurricane
    and the sea claimed him

Barrett was not a sailor
  to take a man from the water
    the sea claimed him too

At noon the storm ceased
  and we heard *The Maisie*'d foundered
    high upon a Mayo strand

The woman came from the forecastle
  she came up alone on deck
    and a great heave cast her out on shore

And another heave came while she drowned
  and put her on her knees
    like a person'd be in prayer

That's the way the people found her
  and the sea never came in
    near that mark no more

John Kerrigan was found
   far down at Achill Sound
     he's buried there

Michael Barrett was taken
   off Murrisk Pier
     he's buried there

Kerrigan's wife was brought from Cross
   home to Inishbofin
     and she's buried there

RICHARD MURPHY

hooker: single-masted fishing smack

SEA TRADE

Eteocles was I, whom hope of gain
In ocean trade lured from a farmer's home;
I crossed the ridges of the Tyrrhene main
   And, ship and all, plunged headlong to my doom,
Crushed by a sudden squall; for different gales
Blow on the threshing-floor, and on the sails.

ISIDORUS

Translated from the Greek by Sir William Marris

LOST AT SEA

From Sparta to Apollo we
Sailed with the first-fruits of the year;
But one night wrecked us in one sea,
And in one grave men laid us here.

SIMONIDES
Translated from the Greek by Arundell Esdaile

TAKE THOUGHT

God by land and sea defend you,
   Sailors all, who pass my grave;
Safe from wreck his mercy send you –
   I am one he did not save.

PLATO
Translated from the Greek by T. F. Higham

WRECKERS,
INVADERS,
PIRATES
AND
PRISONERS

Thus said the rushing raven,
  Unto his hungry mate:
'Ho! gossip! for Bude Haven:
  There be corpses six or eight.
Cawk! Cawk! the crew and skipper
  Are wallowing in the sea:
So there's a savoury supper
  For my old dame and me.'

'Cawk! gaffer! thou art dreaming,
  The shore hath wreckers bold;
Would rend the yelling seamen,
  From the clutching billows' hold.
Cawk! cawk! they'd bound for booty
  Into the dragon's den:
And shout, for "death or duty",
  If the prey were drowning men.'

Loud laughed the listening surges,
  At the guess our grandame gave:
You might call them Boanerges,
  From the thunder of their wave.
And mockery followed after
  The sea-bird's jeering brood:
That filled the skies with laughter,
  From Lundy Light to Bude.

'Cawk! cawk!' then said the raven,
  'I am fourscore years and ten:
Yet never in Bude Haven,
  Did I croak for rescued men. –

They will save the Captain's girdle,
  And shirt, if shirt there be:
But leave their blood to curdle,
  For my old dame and me.'

So said the rushing raven,
  Unto his hungry mate:
'Ho! gossip! for Bude Haven:
  There be corpses six or eight.
Cawk! cawk! the crew and skipper
  Are wallowing in the sea:
O what a savoury supper
  For my old dame and me.'

ROBERT STEPHEN HAWKER

Hennacliff rises to a height of about 454 ft or 138 metres sheer from the
sea at Morwenstow, a cliff-top parish in the north-east corner of Cornwall.
The poet Robert Stephen Hawker was Vicar here in the 19th century,
organized many sea-rescues and gave drowned seamen Christian burial.

The fishermen brothers James and John, both disciples of Jesus, were
given by him the surname 'Boanerges'. In the Bible, this is usually said to
mean 'sons of thunder'. See Luke ix, 54, and also Mark iii, 17.

SONG OF THE CORNISH WRECKERS

Not that they shall, but if they must –
Be just, Lord, wreck them off St Just.

Scythes beneath the water, Brisons,
Reap us a good crop in all seasons.

We would be meek, but meat we lack.
Pile wrecks on Castle Kenidjack.

Our children's mouths gape like a zawn.
Fog, hide the sharp fangs of Pendeen.

You put Your own Son first, Jehovah,
And so do we. Send bread to Morvah.

Crowbar of oceans, stove the wood
Treasure-troves on Gurnard's Head.

Mermaids, Mary-Anne, Morwenna,
Sing them to the crags of Zennor.

Food, Lord, food! Our starving flock
Looks for manna but finds a rock.

Hard land you give us. Mist and stones.
Not enough trees to bury our bones.

To save the drowning we'll risk our lives.
But hurl their ships upon St Ives.

Guide us, when through death we sail,
Past the burning cliffs of Hell.

Soul nor sailor mean we harm.
But our blue sky is their black storm.

D. M. THOMAS

zawn: old Cornish – a slice eaten out of a cliff-face by sea and weather

All the places mentioned are on Cornwall's north-west coast, near Land's End.

In Cornwall, before the days of lighthouses and modern navigational aids, the coasts, seas, and 'races', were so hazardous that a number of ships could confidently be expected to founder without benefit of 'wreckers'. Here, also, to go 'wrecking' still means to salvage (not to *cause* a wreck), or to go beachcombing. But certainly, in earlier times, grindingly poor and isolated communities, with no special sympathy for unknown strangers, looked on a shipwreck almost as a blessing.

O'ER THE WILD GANNET'S BATH

O'er the wild gannet's bath
Come the Norse coursers!
O'er the whale's heritance
Gloriously steering!
With beaked heads peering,
Deep-plunging, high-rearing,
Tossing their foam abroad,
Shaking white manes aloft,
Creamy-neck'd, pitchy-ribb'd,
Steeds of the ocean!

O'er the Sun's mirror green
Come the Norse coursers!
Trampling its glassy breadth
Into bright fragments!
Hollow-back'd, huge-bosom'd,
Fraught with mail'd riders,
Clanging with hauberks,
Shield, spear, and battleaxe,
Canvas-wing'd, cable-rein'd,
Steeds of the Ocean!

O'er the Wind's ploughing field
Come the Norse coursers!
By a hundred each ridden,
To the bloody feast bidden,
They rush in their fierceness
And ravine all round them!
Their shoulders enriching
With fleecy-light plunder,
Fire-spreading, foe-spurning,
Steeds of the Ocean!

GEORGE DARLEY

Norse coursers: swift Viking ships   *ravine*: to dash violently

PIRATE DITTY

Fifteen men on the Dead Man's Chest –
  Yo-ho-ho, and a bottle of rum!
Drink and the devil had done for the rest –
  Yo-ho-ho, and a bottle of rum!

ROBERT LOUIS STEVENSON
From *Treasure Island*

THORKILD'S SONG

There's no wind along these seas,
Out oars for Stavanger!
Forward all for Stavanger!
So we must wake the white-ash breeze,
Let fall for Stavanger!
A long pull for Stavanger!

Oh, hear the benches creak and strain!
(A long pull for Stavanger!)
She thinks she smells the Northland rain!
(A long pull for Stavanger!)

She thinks she smells the Northland snow,
And she's as glad as we to go.

She thinks she smells the Northland rime,
And the dear dark nights of winter-time.

She wants to be at her own home pier,
To shift her sails and standing gear.

She wants to be in her winter-shed,
To strip herself and go to bed.

Her very bolts are sick for shore,
And we – we want it ten times more!

So all you Gods that love brave men,
Send us a three-reef gale again!

Send us a gale, and watch us come,
With close-cropped canvas slashing home!

But – there's no wind on all these seas,
A long pull for Stavanger!
So we must wake the white-ash breeze.
A long pull for Stavanger!

RUDYARD KIPLING

white-ash: an oar made of the light-coloured wood of a particular kind of
   ash tree
reef: part of a sail taken in or rolled up so that less of its area is caught by
   the wind

THE NEGRO'S COMPLAINT

Forc'd from home, and all its pleasures,
   Afric's coast I left forlorn;
To increase a stranger's treasures,
   O'er the raging billows borne.
Men from England bought and sold me,
   Paid my price in paltry gold;
But, though slave they have enroll'd me,
   Minds are never to be sold.

Still in thought as free as ever,
   What are England's rights, I ask,
Me from my delights to sever,
   Me to torture, me to task?
Fleecy locks, and black complexion
   Cannot forfeit nature's claim;

Skins may differ, but affection
   Dwells in white and black the same.

Why did all-creating Nature
   Make the plant for which we toil?
Sighs must fan it, tears must water,
   Sweat of ours must dress the soil.
Think, ye masters iron-hearted,
   Lolling at your jovial boards;
Think how many backs have smarted
   For the sweets your cane affords.

Is there, as ye sometimes tell us,
   Is there one, who reigns on high?
Has he bid you buy and sell us,
   Speaking from his throne the sky?
Ask him, if your knotted scourges,
   Fetters, blood-extorting screws,
Are the means which duty urges
   Agents of his will to use?

Hark! he answers, – Wild tornadoes,
   Strewing yonder sea with wrecks;
Wasting towns, plantations, meadows,
   Are the voice with which he speaks.
He, foreseeing what vexations
   Afric's sons should undergo,
Fix'd their tyrants' habitations
   Where his whirlwinds answer – No.

By our blood in Afric wasted,
   Ere our necks receiv'd the chain;
By the mis'ries we have tasted,
   Crossing in your barks the main;
By our suff'rings since ye brought us

To the man-degrading mart;
All sustain'd by patience taught us
Only by a broken heart:

Deem our nation brutes no longer
Till some reason ye shall find
Worthier of regard and stronger
Than the colour of our kind.
Slaves of gold, whose sordid dealings
Tarnish all your boasted pow'rs,
Prove that you have human feelings
Ere you proudly question ours!

WILLIAM COWPER

the plant for which we toil: includes the sugar-cane
man-degrading mart: slave-market

After this poem, written in 1788, first appeared it was used widely by the
abolitionists or opponents of Negro slavery.

COCK AT SEA

The wooden cage was wedged on the ship's prow
Between sails, vomit, chains that groaned all night.
The grey dawn broke, I heard the sick bird crow
Across the bitter water to the light.

The farm was dancing though that jagged cry –
Tall hay-stack, seed-rich field, barn, hedge and tree,
Cocks that could proudly strut, birds that could fly –
And he a captive of the grinding sea.

No answer from that farm, endless the blue,
Endless the waves, the slaps of salty breath.
He crowed again, the day was rising new
To feed this nightmare in the sleep of death.

C. A. TRYPANIS

BATTLES
AND
ENGAGEMENTS

A BURNT SHIP

Out of a fired ship, which, by no way
But drowning, could be rescued from the flame,
Some men leap'd forth, and ever as they came
Near the foe's ships, did by their shot decay;
So all were lost, which in the ship were found,
   They in the sea being burnt, they in the burnt
     ship drowned.

JOHN DONNE

GOD AND THE SAILOR WE ALIKE ADORE

God and the Sailor we alike adore
But only when in danger, not before:
The danger o'er, both are alike requited,
God is forgotten and the sailor slighted.

JOHN OWEN

RULE, BRITANNIA

When Britain first, at Heaven's command,
   Arose from out the azure main,
This was the charter of her land,
   And guardian angels sung this strain:
     'Rule, Britannia, rule the waves;
     Britons never will be slaves.'

The nations, not so blest as thee
   Must, in their turns, to tyrants fall;

While thou shalt flourish great and free,
　The dread and envy of them all.
　　'Rule', etc.

Still more majestic shalt thou rise,
　More dreadful from each foreign stroke;
As the loud blast that tears the skies
　Serves but to root thy native oak.
　　'Rule', etc.

Thee haughty tyrants ne'er shall tame;
　All their attempts to bend thee down
Will but arouse thy generous flame,
　But work their woe, and thy renown.
　　'Rule', etc.

To thee belongs the rural reign;
　Thy cities shall with commerce shine;
All thine shall be the subject main;
　And every shore it circles, thine.
　　'Rule', etc.

The Muses, still with freedom found,
　Shall to thy happy coast repair:
Blest isle! with matchless beauty crowned,
　And manly hearts to guard the fair:
　　'Rule, Britannia, rule the waves,
　　Britons never will be slaves.'

JAMES THOMSON

Britannia: a poetic and Latin name for Britain; usually shown as a woman
　seated on a globe, and with helmet, shield and trident. The Romans
　depicted Britannia on a coin, and it was first shown on a copper coin in
　Britain during the reign of Charles II
The Muses: the nine Greek sister-goddesses who between them were
　thought to inspire all art and learning

TIME, OFF O' COP'NHAÏG'N

(A Jutlander's account of the Battle of Copenhagen,
Maundy Thursday, 1801)

Time, off o' Cop'nhaïg'n, Nels'n comed an' crep his
    waïy in –
'twor saïme's o' Mond'y Thu'sd'y, on'y fightin' stiddy
    praïyin' –
th' scrappin' start a chu'ch-time, bein' th' bells had
    rung f'r 10;
but that gone 3 an' more, A laïy, 'fore Nels'n said
    amen.
An' we was in ut, all on us – kim fr'm one plaïce, th'
    three –
aboord o' that 'ere *Touchst'n*; there was Jem an' Pete
    an' me.

We'd eat our breakf'st, jes' gone 8, there come a shout
    fr'm Cap'n:
'Now then, yew bors, togither! Shaïke a leg, an' don't
    set napp'n!'
An' all them ships goo saïlin' by an' rootlin' roun'-shot
    in us;
at las' th'r come three all at wunst and laid right clost
    agin' us.
They fired, we fired. Our cap'n – Peter Lass'n wor his
    naïme –
yawled: 'Maïke he païy f'r that 'un!' every time a
    roun'-shot caïme.
Them balls kim flyin' thick as dust an' whistlin' like a
    plover;
we worn't n' more 'n skittleses, th' waïy they bowled us
    over.

An' nigh on noon pore Jem an' Pete rool back'rds on
    th' floor;
A kinder sighed t' m'self, A did: 'Ye 'ont see *them* n'
    more.'

So then we goo on millun', but th' fight got no sense in
    her;
fower had strook a'ready, an' we hadn't had no dinner.
At las' them furriners sim tired o' all that pesky 'splodin',
an' our lootenant mops his brow: 'Belaïy there wi' y'r
    loadin'!' . . .

STEEN STEENSEN BLICHER
Translated from the Danish by R. P. Keigwin

It was during the Battle of Copenhagen that Nelson ignored a signal to
discontinue action with the remark, 'I have only one eye – I have a right
to be blind sometimes'. He then put the telescope to his blind eye and
exclaimed, 'I really do not see the signal!' Losses were heavy: the British,
943 killed and wounded, the Danes between 1600 and 1800.

As a young man serving in the Students' Corps, the poet Blicher lost all
his possessions, including the MS. of a play he had written, during the
bombardment of Copenhagen. Later, he became a country parson and
wrote many stories and poems in the Jutish dialect. In order to give some-
thing of the 'feel' of the original, the translator has rendered the poem in
the dialect with which he happened to be most familiar: that of Essex.

THUS WITH IMAGIN'D WING
OUR SWIFT SCENE FLIES

CHORUS
Thus with imagin'd wing our swift scene flies
In motion of no less celerity
Than that of thought. Suppose that you have seen
The well-appointed king at Hampton pier
Embark his royalty; and his brave fleet
With silken streamers the young Phoebus fanning:
Play with your fancies, and in them behold
Upon the hempen tackle ship-boys climbing;
Hear the shrill whistle which doth order give
To sounds confus'd; behold the threaden sails,
Borne with the invisible and creeping wind,
Draw the huge bottoms through the furrow'd sea,
Breasting the lofty surge. O! do but think
You stand upon the rivage and behold
A city on the inconstant billows dancing;
For so appears this fleet majestical,
Holding due course to Harfleur. Follow, follow!
Grapple your minds to sternage of this navy,
And leave your England, as dead midnight still,
Guarded with grandsires, babies, and old women,
Either past or not arriv'd to pith and puissance:
For who is he, whose chin is but enrich'd
With one appearing hair, that will not follow
Those cull'd and choice-drawn cavaliers to France?

WILLIAM SHAKESPEARE
From *Henry V*

rivage: shore
puissance: great strength; influence

ACTION STATIONS

'Action stations'. Tin hats and apprehension;
Rush to guns and hoses, engine room
And wireless office. Air of tension.
Eyes uplifted and some seawards gazing.
Ears are straining for a distant 'boom',
Or roar of engines. Lips are phrasing
Prayers, maybe, or curse upon the Hun.
Friendly aircraft in the distance loom
And are gone. Minutes pass . . . 'Carry on'.

JOHN WEDGE

THE SEA BATTLE

An American aircraft carrier
and a Gothic cathedral
simultaneously sank each other
in the middle of the Pacific.
To the last
the young curate played on the organ.
Now aeroplanes and angels hang in the air
and have nowhere to land.

GÜNTER GRASS
Translated from the German by Michael Hamburger

VOYAGINGS,
DEPARTURES
AND
HOMECOMINGS

THE SEA IS ASLEEP

The sea is asleep. The calm beloved by the west wind spreads out over the broad water where the ships pass.

No waves beat against the high poops or spew their foam along the shore.

Sailor, burn at the altar a portion of glittering mullet, or a cuttle-fish, or a vocal skaros, to Priapos, lord of ocean and giver of safe harbourage.

Then set out fearlessly on your voyage to the bounds of the Ionian sea.

THEAITETOS
Translated from the Greek by Forrest Reid

vocal skaros: a fish thought by the Ancient Greeks to have a voice; when eaten, it was said to have a most appetizing and savoury taste (not sweet); today, believed by some to be the same as the tropical parrot-wrasse or parrot-fish, which has a particularly strong jaw

The poem is from *The Greek Anthology*, a famous collection written by over 300 poets between the 7th century B.C. and the 10th century A.D.

SAILING WEATHER

The best time for making a voyage is during the fifty days that follow upon the solstice, when summer is drawing to a close. You will not wreck your ship at that season, nor will the sea drown your men, unless Neptune lord of the earthquake sets himself to wreck you, or Jove king of the immortals compasses your destruction, for the issues of good or evil are in their hands. At that season the winds are steady and the sea safe; you can therefore draw your ship into the water in confidence, relying upon the winds, and get your cargo duly within her, but come home again as fast as you can; do not wait for the new wine, nor for the autumn rain and the beginning of winter with the great gales that the South wind raises when it begins to blow after heavy rain in autumn, and makes the sea dangerous. There is also a time in spring when men make voyages; as soon as the buds begin to show on the twigs of a fig-tree about as large as the print of a crow's foot, the sea is fit for sailing, but a voyage at this season is dangerous; I do not advise it, I do not approve of it, for the voyage will be a snatched one, and you will hardly escape trouble of some sort. Nevertheless, men are foolish enough to go voyages even then, for money is the life and soul of us poor mortals, but drowning is a horrible death; I bid you, therefore, think well over all that I have been saying to you.

HESIOD
From *Works and Days*
Translated from the Greek by Samuel Butler

solstice: one of the two occasions in the year (on the longest and shortest days, in June and December) when the sun is farthest from the equator and seems to pause before turning back on its apparent course

ROWING GO THE ROWERS

Rowing go the rowers
In a ship of great delight.
The captain at the helm
The Son of God is Light.
Angels at the oars
Rowed with all their might.
The flag of hope was flying
Lovely to the sight.
The mast was of endurance
Like crystal shining bright.

The sails were stitched with faith
And filled the world with light.
The seashore was serene
With not a wind in flight.

GIL VICENTE
Translated from the Portuguese by Roy Campbell

THE SHORT STRAW

Once on a time a little ship
Went sailing on the sea,
In seven long years not one saw land
Of all her company.

The victuals now were running out
And hunger had them beaten,
So then the sailors all drew lots
To see who would be eaten.

The captain drew the shortest straw:
Cried he: 'O Virgin Mother,
I am the one who's for the pot,
I, and not any other!'

Then up and spake the cabin-boy:
'Captain, give me your lot;
I will be eaten in your stead,
'Tis me now for the pot.

'But ere I die one boon I beg,
Grant me to climb the mast
And over all the ocean wide
To look my very last.'

Up went the boy and far aloft
He gazed around and cried:
'I see the tower of Babylon,
And Barbary t'other side.

'I see a flock of sheep,' he sang,
'Their shepherdess too I see,
And our captain's lovely daughter
Feeding her pigeons three.'

'Well may you sing, brave sailor;
For these good things you tell
You shall have your captain's daughter
And his bonny ship as well.'

ANONYMOUS
Translated from the 16th-century French
by Norma Douglas-Henry

NURSERY RHYME OF
INNOCENCE AND EXPERIENCE

I had a silver penny
    And an apricot tree
And I said to the sailor
    On the white quay

'Sailor O sailor
    Will you bring me
If I give you my penny
    And my apricot tree

'A fez from Algeria
    An Arab drum to beat
A little gilt sword
    And a parakeet?'

And he smiled and he kissed me
    As strong as death
And I saw his red tongue
    And I felt his sweet breath

'You may keep your penny
    And your apricot tree
And I'll bring your presents
    Back from sea.'

O the ship dipped down
    On the rim of the sky
And I waited while three
    Long summers went by

Then one steel morning
    On the white quay
I saw a grey ship
    Come in from sea

Slowly she came
    Across the bay
For her flashing rigging
    Was shot away

All round her wake
    The seabirds cried
And flew in and out
    Of the hole in her side

Slowly she came
  In the path of the sun
And I heard the sound
  Of a distant gun

And a stranger came running
  Up to me
From the deck of the ship
  And he said, said he

'O are you the boy
  Who would wait on the quay
With the silver penny
  And the apricot tree?

'I've a plum-coloured fez
  And a drum for thee
And a sword and a parakeet
  From over the sea.'

'O where is the sailor
  With bold red hair?
And what is that volley
  On the bright air?

'O where are the other
  Girls and boys?
And why have you brought me
  Children's toys?'

CHARLES CAUSLEY

And flew in and out | Of the hole in her side: the lines come from a memory
of the cruiser H.M.S. *Penelope* in the Mediterranean during the Second
World War, so badly holed by bombs and shells that sailors nicknamed
her 'the pepper-pot'

LEGEND

I saw three ships go sailing by,
Over the sea, the lifting sea,
And the wind rose in the morning sky,
And one was rigged for a long journey.

The first ship turned towards the west,
Over the sea, the running sea,
And by the wind was all possessed
And carried to a rich country.

The second turned towards the east,
Over the sea, the quaking sea,
And the wind hunted it like a beast
To anchor in captivity.

The third ship drove towards the north,
Over the sea, the darkening sea,
But no breath of wind came forth,
And the decks shone frostily.

The northern sky rose high and black
Over the proud unfruitful sea,
East and west the ships came back
Happily or unhappily:

But the third went wide and far
Into an unforgiving sea
Under a fire-spilling star,
And it was rigged for a long journey.

PHILIP LARKIN
From *The North Ship*

SO WE AVOIDED THAT ISLAND

SAILOR So we avoided that island
and lay to the sea, searching for a hole in the wind.
At last, by the Grace of God, on the 6th of May,
we passed that terrible Cape,
and sailed north for two months without taking rest.
In those two months we lost twenty-one men
whom we gave to the sea with prayers.
Constrained by our famine
we put in at the Cape Verde Isles,
which were also those of our enemies.
If they had known we were the men of Magellan
they would have seized us from jealousy
and our voyage would have been lost.
But we tricked them, and obtained two boatloads of
  rice.

And here we discovered a strange thing,
for when some asked the day they were told it was
  Thursday,
but by our exact reckoning it was Wednesday with us,
and this was a thing that has now been proved to us,
that by going round the earth, westward with the sun,
we had gained a day.

BEGGAR And when you had gained it, sailor,
what did you do with it?

SAILOR Peace, blind man, for your tongue is as dull
  as your eye.
We left the Cape Verdes
and our journey was nearly done.

We sailed north with a good wind
and the smell of our homes came to us.
Oh, miraculous that smell and those winds of God!
At last, when it pleased heaven,
on Saturday, the 6th of September,
nine months from the Malucos
and three years from the start of our voyage,
we entered the bay of San Lucar.
And that bay of Spain was like pure gold,
and children floated in the streets like angels,
and the white houses of the town glittered with good-
    ness.
So we sailed up the river,
and on the 8th of September
anchored again near the mole of Seville.
And we crept from that tiny ship into the sun,
staring like yellow corpses.
For of that two hundred and sixty men who sailed in
    our five ships,
two hundred and forty-two were lost and drowned and
    murdered –
scattered like studs along the belt of our voyage. . .

We are the eighteen who have come round the world;
we have followed the sun in its setting
over a hundred seas, and have learnt one thing;
that all lands are alike in sin and beauty.
We have come round the world
to walk through these streets of Seville,
barefooted, in shirts and candles –
and this church is the end of our journey.
We have come to say Mass for the living, and for the
    souls of the dead;

but you, blind man, if you could look upon us who are
   left,
would not know whether we lived or died.

BEGGAR Sailor, I do not need to look,
by my ears I know your death is already with you. . .

LAURIE LEE
From *The Voyage of Magellan* (a verse radio play)

island: Mozambique, in East Africa

The Portuguese navigator Ferdinand Magellan (*c.*1480–1521) passed
through the straits called after him in 1520, and so reached the ocean
which he named the Pacific. His (Spanish) expedition was the first to sail
round the world, but he himself died before it completed its journey back
to Spain.

COLUMBUS

To find the Western path,
Right thro' the Gates of Wrath . . .
BLAKE

As I walked with my friend,
My singular Columbus,
Where the land comes to an end
And the path is perilous,
Where the wheel and tattered shoe
And bottle have been thrown,
And the sky is shining blue,
And the heart sinks like a stone,

I plucked his sleeve and said,
'I have come far to find
The springs of a broken bed,
The ocean, and the wind.

I'd rather live in Greece,
Castile, or an English town
Than wander here like this
Where the dunes come tumbling down.'

He answered me, 'Perhaps.
But Europe never guessed
America, their maps
Could not describe the West.
And though in Plato's glass
The stars were still and clear,
Yet nothing came to pass
And men died of despair.'

He said, 'If there is not
A way to China, one
City surpassing thought,
My ghost will still go on.
I'll spread the airy sail.'
He said, 'and point the sprit
To a country that cannot fail,
For there's no finding it.'

Straightway we separated –
He, in his fading coat,
To the water's edge, where waited
An admiral's longboat.
A crew of able seamen
Sprang up at his command –
An angel or a demon –
And they rowed him from the land.

LOUIS SIMPSON

sprit: small boom or pole reaching diagonally from mast to the upper,
outer corner of a fore-and-aft sail

THE EMIGRANT

Going by Daly's shanty I heard the boys within
Dancing the Spanish hornpipe to Driscoll's violin,
I heard the sea-boots shanking the rough planks of the
  floor,
But I was going westward, I hadn't heart for more.

All down the windy village the noise rang in my ears,
Old sea-boots stamping, shuffling, it brought the bitter
  tears,
The old tune piped and quavered, the lilts came clear
  and strong,
But I was going westward, I couldn't join the song.

There were the grey stone houses, the night wind
  blowing keen,
The hill-sides pale with moonlight, the young corn
  springing green,
The hearth nooks lit and kindly, with dear friends good
  to see.
But I was going westward, and the ship waited me.

JOHN MASEFIELD

ONE FOOT ON SEA, AND ONE
ON SHORE

'Oh tell me once and tell me twice
　　And tell me thrice to make it plain,
When we who part this weary day,
　　When we who part shall meet again.'

'When windflowers blossom on the sea
　　And fishes skim along the plain,
Then we who part this weary day,
　　Then you and I shall meet again.'

'Yet tell me once before we part,
　　Why need we part who part in pain?
If flowers must blossom on the sea,
　　Why, we shall never meet again.

'My cheeks are paler than a rose,
　　My tears are salter than the main,
My heart is like a lump of ice
　　If we must never meet again.'

'Oh weep or laugh, but let me be,
　　And live or die, for all's in vain;
For life's in vain since we must part,
　　And parting must not meet again

'Till windflowers blossom on the sea
　　And fishes skim along the plain;
Pale rose of roses, let me be, –
　　Your breaking heart breaks mine again.'

CHRISTINA ROSSETTI

windflowers: wood anemones

BEHOLD THE HOUR, THE BOAT ARRIVE

Behold the hour, the boat arrive;
   Thou goest, the darling of my heart;
Sever'd from thee, can I survive,
   But Fate has will'd and we must part.
I'll often greet the surging swell,
   Yon distant Isle will often hail:
'E'en here I took the last farewell;
   There, latest mark'd her vanish'd sail.'

Along the solitary shore,
   While flitting sea-fowl round me cry
Across the rolling, dashing roar,
   I'll westward turn my wistful eye:
'Happy, thou Indian grove,' I'll say,
   'Where now my Nancy's path may be!
While thro' thy sweets she loves to stray,
   O tell me, does she muse on me!'

ROBERT BURNS

'Clarinda' (Mrs Agnes Craig or MacLehose) was married at 17, and deserted by her husband four years later. Burns, who was the same age as 'Clarinda', met her in Edinburgh in 1787. In 1791, she decided to travel to Jamaica and rejoin her husband. The poem, based on an old song, is a version of one of several sent to her by Burns from Dumfries at this time.

FIDDLER'S GREEN

As I roved by the dock-side one evening so rare,
To view the still waters and take the salt air,
I heard an old fisherman singin' this song,
Oh – take me away boys, me time is not long.

Chorus
Dress me up in me oil-skin and jumper,
– No more on the docks I'll be seen,
Just tell me old ship-mates I'm takin' a trip, mates,
And I'll see you some day in Fiddler's Green.

Now Fiddler's Green is a place I've heard tell
Where fishermen go if they don't go to hell
Where the weather is fair and the dolphins do play
And the cold coast of Greenland is far far away.

The sky's always clear and there's never a gale
And the fish jump on board with the flip of their tail
You can lie at your leisure, there's no work to do
And the skipper's below makin' tea for the crew.

And when you're in dock and the long trip is through
There's pubs and there's clubs and there's lassies there
  too
Now the girls are all pretty and the beer is all free
And there's bottles of rum hangin' from every tree.

I don't want a harp nor a halo, not me
Just give me a breeze and a good rolling sea
And I'll play me old squeeze-box as we sail along
When the wind's in the riggin' to sing me this song.

JOHN CONOLLY

DOUBLETAKE

A sunny afternoon in Wicklow Town,
and suddenly the two men pass,
arguing in quick Greek. Until I see
their ship unloading by the quiet grey quay,

thoughts of past travels weigh me down.
Did last night's raging mountain wind
transplant our cottage to the Cyclades?
Are exiles lighter for such jokes as these?

ALEXIS LYKIARD

Cyclades: a circular group of islands in the Aegean Sea lying round Delos,
which is said to be the birthplace of Apollo and his twin sister Artemis.

DOUBLE NEGATIVE

You were standing on the quay
Wondering who was the stranger on the mailboat
While I was on the mailboat
Wondering who was the stranger on the quay

RICHARD MURPHY

INDEX OF FIRST LINES

INDEX OF AUTHORS

ACKNOWLEDGEMENTS

The editor and publishers wish to thank the following for permission to use copyright material in this collection:

George Harrap & Co. Ltd for 'The Press-Gang' from *A Book of Sea Verse*, ed. R. Hope; Heinemann Educational Books Ltd for 'Blow the Wind Whistling' from *The Idiom of the People*, ed. James Reeves, 'The Saucy Sailor Boy' and 'The Death of Parker' from *The Everlasting Circle*, ed. James Reeves; The Hogarth Press Ltd for 'The Fishermen's Song' from *The Hogarth Book of Scottish Nursery Rhymes*, ed. N. & W. Montgomerie; Faber & Faber Ltd and Random House Inc. for 'On This Island' from *Collected Poems* by W. H. Auden, ed. Edward Mendelson, © 1937 renewed 1965 by W. H. Auden; Faber & Faber Ltd for 'On a Quay by the Sea' and 'The Tides to Me, the Tides to Me from *Runes and Rhymes and Tunes and Chimes* by George Barker; John Murray (Publishers) Ltd and W. W. Norton & Co. Inc. for 'Delectable Duchy' from *A Nip in the Air: Poems* by John Betjeman © 1974 by John Betjeman; Mr George Mackay Brown for 'Fisherman' from *The Storm*; The Hogarth Press Ltd for 'Press-Gang' and 'Beachcomber' from *Poems New and Selected* by George Mackay Brown; Oxford University Press for 'Meeting at Night' and 'Here's to Nelson's Memory!' by Robert Browning from *Browning's Poetical Works*, ed. Ian Jack (1970); The Bodley Head for 'Fishing Boats in Martigues' by Roy Campbell from *Collected Poems*, Vol. II, 'Rowing Go the Rowers' by Gil Vicente, trans. Roy Campbell, from *Collected Poems*, Vol. III, and 'At St Simeon's Shrine I Sat Down to Wait' by Mindinho, trans. Roy Campbell, from *Complete Poems*; Macmillan London Ltd and Charles Causley for 'Angel Hill' from *Collected Poems* and 'Tell Me, Tell Me, Sarah Jane' from *Figgie Hobbin*; Rupert Hart-Davis Ltd and Charles Causley for 'Nursery Rhyme of Innocence and Experience' from *Union Street*; Harvard University Press for 'Now Two Old Salts, Who Knew the Fisher's Trade' by Theocritus, trans. H. H. Chamberlin, from *Late Spring: a Translation of Theocritus* (1936); Penguin Books Ltd for 'There was a Skipper Hailing from Far West', from 'The Prologue' to *The Canterbury Tales* by Geoffrey Chaucer, trans. Nevill Coghill (Penguin Classics, revised edition 1960), © Nevill Coghill 1951, 1958, 1960; Gillian Clarke for 'Foghorns'; John Conolly for 'Fiddler's Green'; Chappell & Co. Ltd for 'Has Anybody Seen Our Ship?' by Sir Noël Coward from *Red Peppers* © 1935 Chappell & Co. Ltd; Cresset Press for 'Summer Beach' from *Collected Poems* by Frances Cornford; Kevin Crossley-Holland for 'I Can Sing a True Song about Myself' from *The Anglo Saxons: The Seafarer*, © 1965, and three riddles from *Storm*, © 1965; Andre Deutsch Ltd and Kevin Crossley-Holland for 'A Beach of Stones' from *The Raingiver*; Jonathan Cape Ltd, Wesleyan University Press and Mrs H. M. Davies for 'The Sea is Loth to Lose a Friend', from 'The Call of the Sea' in *The Complete Poems of W. H. Davies*, © 1963 Jonathan Cape Ltd; Hamish Hamilton Ltd for 'Lament for a Sailor' from *The Fern on the Rock: Collected Poems 1935/65* by Paul Dehn © Dehn Enterprises Ltd, 1965, 1976 (Hamish Hamilton Ltd, London); the Literary Trustees of Walter de la Mare and the Society of Authors as their representative, for 'Captain Lean'; Little, Brown & Co., for 'I Started Early, Took My Dog' from *The Complete Poems of*

Emily Dickinson, ed. Thomas H. Johnson; J. C. Hall and Marie J. Douglas for 'The Sea Bird' from *Complete Poems of Keith Douglas* (O.U.P., 1978); Norma Douglas-Henry for 'The Short Straw'; Edward Arnold (Publishers) Ltd for 'The Shark' by Lord Alfred Douglas; David English for 'Sailing'; The Poetry Society for 'Lost at Sea' by Simonides, trans. G. Arundell Esdaile (from *Poetry Review*, September 1914); Jonathan Cape Ltd and the Estate of Robert Frost for 'Once by the Pacific' from *The Poetry of Robert Frost*, ed. Edward Connery Lathem; Chatto & Windus Ltd for 'Riddle' by John Fuller from *Squeaking Crust*; Mr Michael Gibson and Macmillan, London and Basingstoke, for 'The Parrot' by Wilfred Wilson Gibson from *Collected Poems*; Indiana University Press for 'In Memory of the Circus Ship *Euzkera*' from *The Reckless Spenders*, © 1954 by Walker Gibson (originally appeared in *The New Yorker*); W. S. Graham for 'Shian Bay' and 'Gigha' from *The White Threshold* (Faber & Faber, 1949); Martin Secker & Warburg Ltd and Harcourt Brace Jovanovich Inc. for 'The Sea Battle' from *Selected Poems* by Günter Grass, trans. Michael Hamburger, © 1966 Martin Secker & Warburg Ltd; Jonathan Cape Ltd and Harper & Row Publishers Inc. for Part II of 'Two Songs on Caesaria Beach' from *Poems* by Yehuda Amichai, © 1968, English translation copyright © 1968, 1969 by Assia Gutmann; the Trustees of the Hardy Estate, Macmillan London Ltd, Macmillan Publishing Co. Inc. and Macmillan of Canada Ltd for 'The Sailor's Mother' from *Collected Poems* by Thomas Hardy; Faber & Faber Ltd and Oxford University Press Inc. for 'Synge on Aran' from *Death of a Naturalist* by Seamus Heaney, © 1966 by Seamus Heaney; Oxford University Press for 'To the Mermaid at Zennor' by John Heath-Stubbs from *Selected Poems*; Chatto & Windus Ltd for 'Great Black-backed Gulls' and 'The Cormorant' by John Heath-Stubbs from *A Parliament of Birds*; Oxford University Press for 'Take Thought' by Plato, trans. T. F. Higham, from *The Oxford Book of Greek Verse in Translation*, ed. T. F. Higham and C. M. Bowra (1938); Mrs Laura Huxley, Chatto & Windus Ltd and Harper & Row Publishers Inc. for 'Jonah' (1920) from *The Collected Poetry of Aldous Huxley*, ed. Donald Watt, © 1971 by Laura Huxley; Macmillan London and Basingstoke for 'The Ark' by Elizabeth Jennings from *The Secret Brother*; Basil Blackwell & Mott Ltd for 'Time Off o' Cop'nhaïg'n' by Steen Steenson Blicher, trans. R. P. Keigwin, from *The Jutland Wind*; The National Trust, Methuen & Co. Ltd, Macmillan London and Basingstoke Ltd, the Estate of Mrs George Bambridge and Doubleday & Co. Inc. for ' 'Twas when the Rain Fell Steady' from *The Legends of Evil*, and 'The Changelings', 'The Coiner', 'The Last Chantey' and 'Tin Fish' from *The Definitive Edition of Rudyard Kipling's Verse*; James Kirkup for 'The Sand Artist'; Faber & Faber Ltd for 'Legend' from *The North Ship* by Philip Larkin; William Heinemann Ltd, Laurence Pollinger Ltd, Viking Press and the Estate of the late Mrs Frieda Lawrence Ravagli for 'Little Fish' from *The Complete Poems of D. H. Lawrence*, ed. Vivian de Sola Pinto and F. Warren Roberts, © 1964, 1971 by Angelo Ravagli and C. M. Weekley, Executors of the Estate of Frieda Lawrence Ravagli; Laurie Lee for 'So We Avoided That Island' from *The Voyage of the Magellan*; Norman Levine for 'I Woke This Morning to a Solitary Tern' from *I Walk by the Harbour* (Fiddlehead Poetry Books); The Hogarth Press Ltd and Harold Matson Co. Inc. for 'Just Then Another Event' from *The Aeneid of Virgil* (Book II), trans. Cecil Day Lewis, © 1952 by Cecil Day Lewis; Alexis Lykiard for 'Doubletake' from

ACKNOWLEDGEMENTS

Milesian Fables (Arc Publications), © Alexis Lykiard 1976; The Hogarth Press for 'Uncle Roderick' from *A Man in my Position* by Norman MacCraig; Jonathan Cape Ltd and Roger McGough for 'Newsflash' from *In the Glassroom*, © Roger McGough; Oxford University Press for 'Wreck of the Raft' by Homer, trans. J. W. Mackail from *The Odyssey of Homer* (1932); Alasdair Maclean for 'Fishing' from *Poetry Introduction* (Faber & Faber); Faber & Faber Ltd and Oxford University Press Inc. for 'The Lugubrious, Salubrious Seaside' from *The Collected Poems of Louis MacNeice*, ed. E. R. Dodds, © The Estate of Louis MacNeice 1966; Wes Magee for 'Sunday Morning' from *Poetry Introduction II* (Faber & Faber); The Society of Authors as the literary representative of the Estate of John Masefield and Macmillan Publishing Co. Inc. for 'A Ballad of Sir Francis Drake', and 'Porto Bello', © 1936, renewed 1964 by John Masefield), 'Posted as Missing' and 'The Emigrant', (©1912 Macmillan Publishing Co. Inc., renewed 1940 by John Masefield), 'The Lemmings' (© 1920, renewed 1948 by John Masefield), and 'Sea-Change' (© 1916, renewed 1944 by John Masefield), all from *Poems* by John Masefield; Andre Deutsch Ltd and Mr Dom Moraes for his translation of 'Shell to Gentlemen' from *The Brass Serpent* by Tom Carmi (1964); Edwin Morgan and Edinburgh University Press for 'Boats and Places' from *The Second Life*; Faber & Faber Ltd and Harper & Row Publishers Inc. for 'Pat Cloherty's Version of *The Maisie*' and 'Double Negative' from *High Island*, © 1974 by Richard Murphy; Mr Peter Newbolt for 'Drake's Drum' by Sir Henry Newbolt; George G. Harrap & Co. Ltd for 'Messmates' by Sir Henry Newbolt from *Harrap Book of Sea Verse*, ed. R. Hope; Brian Patten for 'The Value of Gold to Sailors'; Martin Secker & Warburg Ltd for 'Crayfish Facts 1–4' from *The Nightowl's Dissection* by William Peskett; Jonathan Cape Ltd and the Estate of William Plomer for 'Archaic Apollo' from *Collected Poems*; J. M. Dent & Sons for 'Waterfront Ballad' by John Pudney; William Heinemann Ltd for 'Stones by the Sea' from *The Wandering Moon* by James Reeves; Oxford University Press for 'The Black Pebble' from *The Blackbird in the Lilac* by James Reeves (1952); Faber & Faber Ltd for 'H.M.S. *Hero*' by Michael Roberts from *Collected Poems*; Mr W. S. Gilbert for 'The Sea is Asleep' by Theaitetos, trans. Forrest Reid; Alan Ross and Eyre/Methuen for 'Off Brighton Pier', from *Poems 1942–67*; A. L. Rowse for 'Charlestown Harbour', Bantam Books Inc., Soledad Salinas de Marichal and Jaime Salinas for 'The Shore' by Pedro Salinas, English translation by Willis Barnstone reprinted from *Modern European Poetry*, © 1966 Bantam Books Inc.; Michael Schmidt for 'A Hermit's Dream', © Michael Schmidt (Carcanet Press Ltd) 1978; Oxford University Press Inc. for 'But Ino of the Slim Ankles had seen him' from *The Odyssey of Homer*, trans. T. E. Shaw, © 1932 by Bruce Rogers, renewed 1960 by A. W. Lawrence; James Simmons for 'The Sea'; Oxford University Press and Harcourt Brace Jovanovich Inc. for 'Colombus' by Louis Simpson from *Selected Poems*, © 1961 Louis Simpson; Methuen & Co. Ltd for 'Follow the Sea', 'A Channel Rhyme' and 'A Saint of Cornwall' by C. Fox Smith from *Sea Songs and Ballads 1917–1923*; William Heinemann Ltd for 'The Moonwuzo's Sea-Song' from *Old Merlaine* by Cara Lockhart Smith; James MacGibbon, Executor, and Oxford University Press Inc. for 'Mrs Arbuthnot' from *Collected Poems of Stevie Smith*, © Stevie Smith 1937, 1938, 1942, 1950, 1957, 1962, 1966, 1971, 1972: © James MacGibbon 1975 (Allen Lane); Harper & Row Publishers Inc. for 'Lobsters in the Window' from *After Experience* by

ACKNOWLEDGEMENTS

W. D. Snodgrass, © 1963 by W. D. Snodgrass (originally appeared in *The New Yorker*); Faber & Faber Ltd and Random House Inc. for 'Word', © 1948 by Stephen Spender (originally appeared in *The New Yorker*), from *Selected Poems* by Stephen Spender; Macmillan London and Basingstoke for 'Discovery' from *Collected Poems of Sir John Squire*; Oxford University Press for 'Song at the Turning of the Tide' from *The Apple Barrel* by Jon Stallworthy (1974); Mrs Iris Wise, Macmillan London and Basingstoke, The Macmillan Company of Canada Ltd and Macmillan Publishing Co. Inc. for 'The Shell'(© 1916 Macmillan Publishing Co. Inc., renewed 1944 by James Stephens) and 'Seumas Beg', from *Collected Poems*; Anne Stevenson for 'North Sea off Carnoustie' (the *New Review* 1975 and 'Enough of Green', Oxford University Press, 1977); Penguin Books Ltd for 'The Whale' from *Medieval English Verse*, trans. Brian Stone (Penguin Classics, 1964), © Brian Stone 1964; George Tardios for 'Sea-Signs' from P.E.N. anthology *New Poems 1976* (Hutchinson); D. M. Thomas for 'Song of the Cornish Wreckers'; Faber & Faber Ltd and Mrs Myfanwy Thomas for 'The Child on the Cliffs' from *Collected Poems 1949*; Rupert Hart-Davis/Granada Publishing Ltd for 'The Sea' and 'Harbour' from *Young and Old* by R. S. Thomas; Oxford University Press for 'Stone Speech' by Charles Tomlinson from *Written on Water* (1972); Faber & Faber Ltd for 'Cock at Sea' by C. A. Trypanis from *The Cocks of Hades*; Chris Wallace-Crabbe and Angus & Robertson Ltd for 'Littoral'; Mrs Vernon Watkins for 'The Heron' from *Selected Poems 1930–1960* (Faber & Faber); Mr J. F. N. Wedge for 'Action Stations' from *More Poems from the Forces*.

For suggestions and assistance in the compilation of this anthology, the editor wishes to thank particularly Mr Jonathan Barker, Poetry Librarian, Arts Council of Great Britain; Mr G. M. Gidley; Mr and Mrs W. G.Morton; Mr Brian Payne, Popular Music Librarian, BBC; Mr P. A. S. Pool; Mr R. N. J. Tamplin; Miss Elizabeth R. Ziman, United States Library (University of London Library); The British Music Hall Society; The Performing Right Society Ltd; Mrs Treld Bicknell, Miss Janice Brent, Mrs Doreen Scott and Miss Felicity Trotman of Penguin Books Ltd; the Librarians and staff of the Cornwall County Library (Truro and Launceston), in particular Mrs Hazel Martin and Miss Rhona Cowling.

Every effort has been made to trace copyright but if any omissions have been made please let us know and acknowledgements will be made in the next edition.